Where There's Love

Betty Lowrey

To order additional copies of this book, contact:
Bookwhip
1-855-339-3589
www.bookwhip.com

Though I speak with the tongues of men and of angels, and have not
love, I am become as a sounding brass or a tinkling cymbal.
1 Corinthians 13:1

WHERE THERE'S LOVE

The listing on the bulletin board at the outskirts of town explained this would be an endeavor by Federal Government and local communities to come together to aid the flooded town that bore no entrance.

Evan considered the source; but the pastor had assured him, this reprieve from small town life, hot with lack of air conditioning, was real. Tomorrow he would arrive with others selected to participate. They were the unfortunate. Swayed by the pastor he had signed up and wished since then that he had not.

* * * * * *

He sat on the first pew in the church auditorium, staring at the replica of Jesus on the cross. Perhaps he was a bit precarious to sit there considering the agony Christ felt on that cross. His own life had not called for extraordinary treats; it had offered those elusive hard to reach advantages and then came the one he signed on for now. The love of music to make each day better as he considered its melodic sound, might seem a bit much for one seeking solitude and contentment as was he but when he showed them his handiwork, their response was a shock that anyone could appreciate his effort that much.

He acknowledged apprehension did come with the territory of needing someone. From strange beginnings, Evan groomed himself, the truth of his situation puzzling. When his mother died giving birth that was the beginning. Now he wondered, would his prayer be answered? That was the reason he allowed himself to join in this small town's retreat that could lead to a month or more stay if he was chosen. Jobs were limited to the skill of the participant. Evan was well trained in work.

He was studying a writer who believed each person is born to a certain moment, for some it might mean great claim to wealth or fame while others might long for the more simple, someone who cared, a person who gave hugs and smiles that cured hearts... yes, Evan had his longings as the next person... and this was his opportunity to taste a life of other people's joy in order to shape his future accordingly. If he could set aside his pride, if that was what it was, a private dislike of baring himself to others.

Sighing heavily he glanced around at the others. None proved worldly, only a group of people who had lost their homes and nearly lost their lives when the damn broke and flooded where they lived. It would take a person with a risky spirit to bring them into their homes again. He prayed for a shack on the outside rather than live in the most spacious opulent room one might find. Who was he to ask so much?

His eyes lingered momentarily on the girl in the old fashioned attire. Uncomfortable, she gave him a slight smile and looked away. Her parents, no doubt, were the two sitting beside her. Dressed from the forties, they wore austere faces and if they had ever smiled it must have been on rare occasion. Still, the girl could be attractive, given the chance. Enchanted, at the sound of her soft voice, the mystery of why her hair was wound at the base of her neck into a bun of sorts, comparable to the one her mother wore, he wondered her story. They would be chosen to a certain home with a need for their skill and possibly he would not see her after this day. But now it was time to learn who your guest host would be. Down the way the old man wearing a ship's captain's hat made a gesture there was a spot for him by her. He wondered did he dare be so bold as to seek her out and sit by her. She interested him. Why?

For some reason he listened to hear her name. "Jewel," the church attendant stepped close to her parents. "Oh, I see, you two have homes already, but you don't?" The young woman shook her head. "Then I know where you will fit in nicely, with the Gates; they have two sets of twins and Ruthie."

* * * * * * *

Uncomfortable, Jewel studied the other occupants of the room. Everyone was nice enough, but she was not used to being under such close scrutiny. In all fairness, her parents would never have taken strangers into their home without a check of their background. And yet, here they sit like refugees from another country, all because the damn broke and forced them off their property. Only the promise of wages eased the hurt of losing all of their personal items for they prayed the water would recede.

She supposed she would remember the pure picture held in her mind of the man about her age in the faded blue shirt and pants. Her father would have said he needed a haircut. She liked his hair that curled onto his shirt collar. She couldn't help but wonder if he noticed the outdatedness of her clothing, and the fact that in her out dated clothing she appeared to have stepped from another era.

* * * * * * *

Pastor Joe walked around the room, slowly observing the people. They were a bit nervous and rightly so, their homes under water, possessions gone or damaged, with little warning. They could not pack and reach safety; in most cases they made an escape to higher ground. The Cape became higher ground.

* * * * * * *

He listened to the musicians warming up in the room down the hall and he longed to join them but they wouldn't know him. He escaped with one instrument unless the others he made were secure up on the hill with his old truck; the two possessions he considered worthy of saving. What would Da say, he wondered. His father succumbed a year past and he missed him every day and amazing as it seemed, he missed her, too. On her death bed she declared she loved him and was sorry for the terrible mess of life they'd shared, much of it her doing. Evan's heart bled with anger and hurt combined. It could have been different. Da was a good man but he had allowed the farce they lived to survive his own lifetime.

* * * * * *

"Young man," Pastor Joe tried to gain his attention. "Young man? They called your name. You don't want to be passed over." He sighed heavily. "I know this is embarrassing but these are good natured, caring people. You won't have any worries with the family you received. I'll see you here on the North field at four tomorrow evening if the Graves don't have you tied up with something to do."

Hoping that was a figure of speech, Evan rose to follow the group. "Excuse me, would you have any idea which way I should go?" He grinned mischievously. "I'm afraid I've become lost."

"Exciting times, Mate," the fellow who professed being a ship's captain was holding court, looking for mates to run the ship. "Next stop," He stopped, scratched his head for a time and then asked. "Does anyone know if they could arrange a cot for me to sleep on tonight? I'll be on my way, tomorrow."

Evan wondered if the congregation of Christ Church knew what it was getting in to taking in complete strangers? The old gentleman was so addled he thought he was going on a ship and was trying to solicit workers. "Listen, Sonny," he said, "In this bag I've me own clothes, my Bible and me very own trusty violin."

"Oh," that interested Evan. "When you have time I'd love to see the instrument."

"No time like now," the old fellow said and stopped right where he was, to take out the violin. Evan took it in his hands, examined the piece as a whole, and then ran his fingers along the grain of wood. "Spruce?" The old man nodded. "Rosewood for the back instead of maple?" A sparkle appeared in the old man's eyes. "It was a pretty piece of wood and the Maple had no burl, just solid the color of honey. You want that glow in the wood that shows life and that's what we have here. Beneath the rosewood you should see the fire's glow. Most maple has that glow but this one, Rosewood is as descriptive as its name."

"May I?" Evan placed the bow, allowing his arm distance but control and as he pulled the bow across the strings the lonely sound of a woman's crying filled the air. Closing his eyes he felt the violin resting upon his shoulder and wondered that it was there, he had spent the last two nights in a rented hotel room, so great was his concentration tonight the strings brought forth what seemed more a woman's cry from pain. Determined to last this most crucifying ordeal, he changed songs slipping into what his step mother would have liked. And when at last the pastor returned for him, he saluted the pastor, the old captain and whoever had filled the gap in his absence. It appeared no one was keeping track of time.

Pastor Joe, weary to the bone, had been on his feet all day, and yet, hearing the violin music felt a tremor of sort run through his being and his feet felt a rhythm that wanted to dance, while at first his heart had spoken of sorrow but the music now was of happier times. Whoever was playing the instrument knew how, and he had a fleeting thought they were either well educated or blessed with talent. By the time he returned, the violin was out of sight and possibly who played it.

CHAPTER 1

Pastor Joe stepped to the pulpit. "I was glad when they said," he began and the congregation chorused, "Let us go in to the house of the Lord." He was beaming. "Here it is mid-winter and we have high attendance today." Everyone clapped. "I can see you were all ready to get out of the house. Right?"

Daniel was basking in the joy everyone was feeling. It seemed they were all of one accord. "Yes," he whispered to Ellen and as he did he saw Ruthie, sitting on the other side of Ellen, wearing an expression he had come to know meant she was *seeing* something he and the others did not see. He gave Ellen a light nudge and fixed his eyes toward Ruthie.

"Oh, my," she whispered back. "I hope this is good and not bad." Their attention returned to Pastor Joe.

"Josiah was eight years old when he began to reign, and he reigned in Jerusalem one and thirty years. And he did that which was right in the sight of the Lord, and walked in the ways of David his father and declined neither to the right hand nor the left. For in the eight year of his reign while he was yet young, he began to seek after the God of David his father."

Daniel stole a glance to Ruthie and saw she was smiling and he began to relax.

As usual all the friends met to share lunch at the nearest restaurant. It was there they rehashed the past and caught up on the present. Ellen ask Anne if she was ready for a speaking appointment the next day and Anne confessed she was a bit nervous and she had ask God to take care of it. Ruthie, as usual was sitting with the younger children. It seemed she had a calming influence on them but Ruthie was listening.

Arriving home, Daniel took the twins to their rooms to change clothes and Ellen followed Ruthie to hers.

"May I come in, Sweetums?" Surprised, Ruthie smiled and reached for her mother's hand while they sit on her bed. "Sweetheart, do you have anything you want to share?"

"You know, don't you?" Ruthie's eyes were dark with the mystery she always felt when she knew God was telling her something. "Did you see me in church when it happened?"

"No, Daddy saw you. Do you want to tell me?"

"I think it's good, Momma but I don't understand it. I've never seen this man before."

"Can you describe him?"

"He is tall as Daddy but he's thin, you know his clothes fit loose." She thought a moment. "His face is thin, but his eyes," She shook her head, "maybe I mean clear and look right into a person." A troubled expression came over her face, "He stares through things and sometimes he's sad and his hair is like sometimes when daddy gets busy and skips a haircut and this man wears a light blue shirt and pants."

"Is he a good man?"

"Yes, but he's sad." Ruthie and her mother stared at each other. "I don't know why he's sad. But Momma I saw Anne, too. Someone was trying to take something away from her."

Ellen sensed Ruthie was troubled. "Is there anything I should do?" She sighed. "Sweetums, we may have this gift God gave us but I don't think he wants us to worry, or he would not have given us scripture that tells us we cannot change anything by spending our time fretting."

"It's all right, Momma. I was worrying until Pastor Joe read the scripture about the boy becoming king when he was eight years old. That helped, Momma, because I always wonder what God expects from me being seven years old."

"What part helped you, Sweetums?"

"Sometimes it's hard to tell people what Jesus wants, but I think that's what he meant when he said the boy that was king declined neither to the right nor the left. He meant he did right or said what was right, didn't he?" Ellen's heart filled with gratitude that God had granted Ruthie wisdom to understand.

"I think you are right, and he sought after the God of his father; just as you seek God, Ruthie." Ellen hugged her daughter. "If you ever want to talk, you can talk to me or Daddy." Ruthie smiled. "Let's remember to say a prayer for Anne. She is speaking tomorrow at the Ladies Seminar."

"Thank goodness, Momma, I was afraid for Anne." Ellen was leaving the room when Ruthie called. "Momma, he is very sad. He has suffered a lifetime of great loss and all he wants is to be loved."

ANNE

She sit through the roll call of important members and those who held office and her thoughts were drawn to a time when she and Ellen were waiting for an important test to begin and she was so nervous she began to shake and from across the aisle a hand reached to squeeze hers and a voice said, "Let your mind settle, take a deep breath and you are going to do just fine." That was Ellen. Now it was her turn.

"You would have to understand what we have been through," Anne said, staring out over the sea of faces attending the Change Your Life Seminar. "We went from young couple crazy in love to divorced with drama." She smiled. "When I say drama, I truly mean drama and trauma." She saw a young woman waving her hand. "Yes, did you have a question?"

"I didn't understand what happened to you in the accident when you went into coma and your ex-husband came to see you in the hospital every day. I think if I were divorced I wouldn't want my ex there. Did he feel responsible or maybe guilty?"

"Perhaps both," Anne replied. "I had returned our son to my ex and he was not at all happy. Conditions outside were bordering on a horrible ice storm with the roads becoming dangerous to travel and still I had to return to where I was staying because I was a nursing student with class the next day. The driver of an eighteen wheeler had lost control of his truck on the over-pass, which careened into a second vehicle that was pushed over the guard rail of the interstate bridge and that vehicle landed on my car as I waited below for the light to change. Needless to say, I was pressed inside a mass of twisted metal, shattered glass and had to be cut free to be taken to the hospital."

"Were you aware of what was happening?"

"I don't know exactly when I lost consciousness but I must have been awake in the beginning, because I do remember my thoughts were with our little boy, Andy, who was a toddler then."

"You are an amazing woman," another voice from the audience proclaimed. "I don't think if it should happen that I could take in my husband's love child with another woman. Why or how could you do that?"

"There was a time I could not have, but the circumstance demanded immediate attention and I knew Andrew would be so torn in how to treat the situation because he did not know she had given birth to his child." Anne paused to remember. "First you would have to remember we had finally worked out a lot of the problems that caused us to divorce and decided we truly loved each other. Unknown to me, for some time the mother of Adeline had been trying to get enough courage to come to me. She was dying of cancer and on most days she was lucid, but then there were days she was filled with remorse that she would miss so many first happenings with her child. She and I had not known a good relationship. The one time we met, she was high on drugs and practically fell out of the car. This was after our divorce. Andrew came to pick up our son and I was devastated allowing Andy getting into the car. She confided the afternoon that we met she had become pregnant during the last days of their being together and never told him, for fear he would claim Addy also. I had no idea she had a daughter or that her little girl would one day come to be a part of our family."

"Do you love little Addy as much as your son, or do you find there is a difference?"

Searching for the owner of the voice, Anne found her on the back row, a very well dressed woman and immediately Anne felt there was more to the question; somehow God was cautioning her to be careful in answering.

Smiling, Anne replied, "I do. Addy has brought us farther in our desire to build a family according to God's principals. Andrew and I lost several years putting our family back together. Now, we try very hard to remember how much God loved us to allow us to raise Addy because her mother could have given her to someone else and we would never have known her love, or known Andrew had a daughter."

"How did you and the little girl's mother arrive at the arrangement for you and your husband to take her?"

"For several months when I would stop for gas, I noticed this car with the little girl in it and I would think is this coincidence that we should be here at the same time each week. It was just a fleeting thought but the little girl always waved at me and then there was the day she managed to get loose from her car seat and was out in traffic and I saw her and ran after her. It was one of those situations you don't stop to think you just act and I pulled her out of the path of a big truck whose driver could not have seen her and in so doing her mother and I came face to face and recognized each other. But to answer your question, God gave me an insight into her mother heart and I felt her sadness and that she had a need."

"What happened after that was it long until you took Addy?"

"No. We both forgot the laws of the land. I took her home with me that evening because her mother insisted. She came fully prepared, should there be an encounter between the two of us; she had Addie's clothes, her cup and favorite toy, even a car seat and her bedding, thinking to keep her in something familiar. It was a human act orchestrated by God. Her friend told Andrew and I she returned home at peace that evening saying she had given Addy into our hands, but she was weak. They put her to bed. She expressed her satisfaction and asked them to stand by us if anything was ever questioned. Addy's mother died that night."

The room was filled with murmurings. There were a few ladies who shed tears. "Were you able to attend the mother's funeral?" One of those wiping away tears stood to ask her question. "I would think that was very hard to do."

The coordinator of the session arose and come to stand with Anne. "Thank you, Mrs. Graves, for sharing what must have been a very traumatic time of your life. You don't have to answer that. We will dismiss this session that all may continue to the next speaker in room 34 just down the hall."

Anne stepped down from the platform and went to the young woman who had asked the question. Taking her hand, she replied, "I don't mind. Yes, we went and we took Addy. It was the least we could do, her mother had entrusted into our care a child she loved more than life. We went to pay respect and in some small way show our appreciation that she would trust us to raise Addy."

The young woman opened her arms and pulled Anne into an embrace. "God bless you," she said. The moment was touching and brought the other ladies to their feet. Anne was standing in a position to see the back row. The well-dressed lady was gone.

* * * * * * *

Andrew arrived home as Anne was carrying Addy into the house.

"How'd it go?" He bussed a kiss on Addy's cheek and peered around her to plant one on Anne's lips. "Here, let me take the pumpkin. Do you want her to stay asleep?" With a free hand he tousled Andy's hair. "How're you, Buddy?" Andy grinned. "Still not talking, huh?" Andrew leaned down to kiss his son. "I love you, son."

"Love you, too, Daddy."

"So?" They were inside, Anne unloading the diaper bag on to the counter top, slipping her jacket off and her feet out of the high heels she thought she must wear. Now she glanced at Andrew still holding Addy.

"You can set her down, if we are going to church, tonight. If we're not, lay her in her bed." She waited to see what he would say.

"You first. How was your speech? Did you change lives?"

Anne's first thought was of the woman who had slipped away before the others and she wondered why she felt unrest when she remembered the woman's question. Shrugging away the feeling, she replied, "I guess it was all right. Heaven knows the attendance was good and why do you suppose that would be?"

"Did you touch on the adoption subject?"

"No, they ask me not to, there were parents present in the session before me that were going to discuss their experience with adoption and they didn't want a repeat." She glanced down the hall where Andy had disappeared and smiled when she heard him start up the toy train he had received for Christmas.

"What other topics were on the agenda?" Instead of laying Addy down, Andrew had settled into the leather rocker with her head on his shoulder. "I love to hold this little moppet. Andy grew up too quick. Now he thinks he's a big boy and is embarrassed to sit on my knees."

"You've turned into an adoring daddy, Daddy." Anne grinned. "I was grilled pretty good today, myself, but right now, are we attending church tonight? I need to decide on a quick meal if we are."

Andrew sighed. "I know we're all tired, but I think we should since Pastor Joe asked everyone to be there. You know they are assigning families willing to take in the homeless…" eyebrows raised, a question hanging between them, he said, "where would we put someone that will stay a month, if necessary, until they find a home for them?"

"The question was raised whether we would be putting our family in danger taking in an unknown stranger, even if Pastor Joe and the committee have chosen the ones considered low risk. I don't know."

"They're probably no more dangerous than some of the characters I ran with before we met."

"Don't remind me." Anne was tying an apron over her skirt and blouse. "I'll brown some beef and fix noodles, if I have a jar of sauce….yes, I do…and we'll have spaghetti. Lay her down, Daddy, and you can make tea and set the table." She listened to Andrew's groan. "You can hold her when we come home." Again, the lady came to her mind and the uneasy feeling she'd had, but that was silly, no need to worry Andrew. If those ladies only knew how domesticated her handsome lawyer husband had become. For a second, the terrible times they'd experienced flit through her mind, but that was then.

"You're quiet." Andrew had set the table, made the tea and filled the glasses with ice. "Do you want Andy to drink milk?" She nodded. "What is it, babe, is something bothering you?"

"Not bothering, just remembering, I don't know why," she met his gaze with troubled eyes. "The ladies ask a number of questions and one of the first one's was had we experienced a life threatening situation? Don't ask me why…the name of the Ladies Day Seminar was Change Your Life and they handed out forms for questions those attending wanted to ask. I found myself telling them about the wreck I was in that caused the coma and briefly touched on Andy's being in a hit and run accident where he, too, was in coma."

"Well, that was traumatic. That always reminds me of Harper Gipson, sinking right down beside me on that dirty bathroom floor and praying the saving grace of Jesus down on me when I was distraught thinking we were losing our boy and I truly think we would have if not for the prayers sent up."

"Which brings us full circle," Anne was draining liquid from the pot full of spaghetti noodles. "When we are so blessed, how can we say no to someone coming to stay with us?"

"Where would we put them?" Andrew was pouring milk into Andy's cup. "What do you have in mind?" He turned when she gave a smothered laugh. "Aw, Babe, it's not even finished and I want the use of it first." She shrugged as she pursed her mouth in that mischievous way he'd grown accustomed to when she knew he wasn't going to be really gung-ho on some situation. "It would push me to finish it." Andrew pulled into the church drive, noting only a dozen or so cars present. "Something tells me the people are afraid to attend; Pastor Joe just might talk them into something they don't want to do."

The windows of Christ Church were aglow, the beveled edges of the stained figures twinkling in the night. "I hadn't noticed that before," Anne said, "See around the window edges, the light turns to prisms. Is that a good sign?"

"Depends on what you need a sign for," he stole a glance, "have you laid out a fleece about something? If it's whether I finish my office, or not..." he stared hard at the stained glass windows, noting you really could not see inside the church, only a glow of certain colors. "If you think I'm happy to finish all that beautiful grained wood and then put some stranger off the street in my work of art..." He stopped speaking, "I know, I know I should be ashamed but Anne, I've looked forward to having my own space at home since we took my office in the house and made it a guest room after Addy came."

She laid a hand on his arm. "Don't give it another thought. I understand and there will be others to take them in. Maybe you and I can supply dinner now and then for some of the busier homes. You think?"

Andrew helped Andy out of his booster seat while Anne collected Addy. He thought about the church windows, he was comparable. He knew what was inside but a stranger looking at him didn't. Wasn't that what Brother Joe stressed to his congregation over and over? "You have a light inside you, supplied by the heavenly father, you are different, let that light shine that others will see it."

The first song was being sung by the time they left the children in the nursery. "There's a light in the window shining for me, all my sins are forgiven, the Lord I did seek, when the storms of life batter my soul, the light in the window reminds me, my life is made whole...Oh, child you're forgiven, I heard Jesus say, you were lost in temptation, now there's a new way, it's the light in the window, you're forgiven today." Andrew sneaked a glance at Anne, her heart pure as she sang and he wondered that things were stacking up against him. If Pastor Joe read a passage on light, he knew his new office was a goner.

"Open your bibles to Matthew chapter five," Pastor Joe waited for the rustle of pages turning, "Now, let's read verse five together, "Even so, let your light shine before men; that they may see your good works and glorify your Father who is in heaven." He let his gaze roam across those present, "Remember, Jesus said you are the light of the world, a city set on a hill cannot be hidden. And he explained why those words are important. Other people are observing." He smiled as he closed his Bible. "How appropriate those words tonight as we discuss the taking into our hearts and our homes those who have been left homeless, without funds until the government can serve each person, and until then they stand in need of a place to lay their head. Those on our list are able bodied persons who have stated they are willing to do tasks you will provide in order to help you as you help them."

The remainder of the service went quickly, but Andrew couldn't really repeat what was said, other than he and Anne would welcome a young man in his twenties, whose home had been washed away when the hillside had caved in and the waters had become a roaring deluge around his hillside home. Less than fifty miles from the Cape, it was almost unbelievable such a parody could happen but it had. Andrew reached for Anne's hand and slipped the paper with the young man's description from her fingers. "He's single," she whispered. "Has some college, lives alone, no family and plays the guitar. I wonder if he salvaged the guitar, it states everything was lost except a late model Ford truck that was stuck on the nearest hill and he hadn't time to get it out of the mud. Isn't that a coincidence?" She was staring at Andrew. "I thought we weren't going to participate, and then you hold your hand up and we are."

"You can't beat city hall," he replied. Anne was confused.

CHAPTER 2

ELLEN

She stood at the sink, her hands in soapy dishwater, hearing the hammers tapping away on the new house down the street. Her thoughts were elsewhere as the house under construction changed on a daily basis. She had been there once. The house plan was different than any she had seen but no one was there to explain it. It was to be a three member family.

"You're quiet over there." Hearing Dan's voice brought her around.

"I was wondering if there will be children in the family that's building down the street and I was thinking about ......" Dan wasn't paying attention and interrupted.

"Don't think so. I heard its three spinster sisters."

"Does that necessarily mean they are elderly?"

"I have no idea. Did you speak with Anne or Andrew?" Daniel glanced up from sorting newspapers. "I know I saw an article I need in one of these throw outs. Have you trashed any? It could have been thrown away."

"No, not yet and no I didn't speak with either of the Graves but we waved at each other across the room." Ellen replied. "Anne did a speaking arrangement today, for the Women's Seminar, I hope it went well." The phone rang and she answered it.

"Hey, we were just talking about you two. I thought you were not going to take in..." She laughed, "You mean Andrew had a change of heart. So who did you get?" Ellen listened. "A man." She turned to watch Daniel discarding old newspapers that had piled up. "Actually, we have a young woman, younger than us, I think. Her name's Jewel, not married. Oh, really? His name is Jacob…yeah; we did do that name study. Protector of God? That's nice." She laughed, "No, I don't know what Jewel stands for, I'd think it is self-explanatory."

Ellen studied the article Dan placed in front of her. "Yeah, thanks for calling. Yes, I'll look it up, now I'm curious." She read the article he offered. "How to make your guest feel comfortable?" A chuckle bubbled up in her chest. "With two sets of twins, I'm not sure Jewel will feel comfortable but she will be aptly entertained."

"Do you feel there's reason for concern, bringing strangers into our home?" Daniel rose to pick up the stack of papers. "You want these in the wastepaper can or will it be too heavy to carry?"

"That's fine. I was wondering how to answer your question. I think we have to experience it. Maybe we will be getting a good quiet person; I know the kids will enjoy her being with us." Ellen yawned. "I think I'm going to bed. Today seemed to have more hours than usual." Daniel gave her a worried glance.

"I'm okay," she said. She felt him tap her on the shoulder and turned.

"I don't know what I'd do if I lost you. It hasn't been a year since you finished treatment. You've got to rest more." He held her as she let herself sink into the comfort of his body. "I realized later that I interrupted you. Were you going to tell me what you have planned for next week?"

"Let's see, Saturday we sell cookies down town and the next Monday Jewel arrives. I'm not going anywhere."

"We don't know that." He held her attention, not speaking, simply staring into her eyes which said more than any words he could string together. "More rest. Less outside assignments until your year of recuperation has passed."

"Yes, doctor Dan." On tiptoe she kissed him, as her eyes glistened with tears. "To think I met you in a shoe store." She grinned. "Size twelve, I believe." He dipped her as though they were dancing. "I give." She said. "But that wasn't it, either."

"So this Monday our house guest, Janice, will arrive and our life changes again."

"Jewel. Think of your watch, if it were in the olden days, it might have jewels in it, but never Janice."

"So what were you thinking that I interrupted and now my interest is really peaked."

"It was what Ruthie said after church Sunday. She mentioned someone taking something from Anne."

"Yeah, I've been thinking about that too. Only time will tell. She's special, our Ruthie."

A WEEK LATER

DOROTHY AND HARPER

"Harper Gipson," Dorothy stared at the plate of cookies she had baked for the Ladies Sweet Shop they were holding down town the next day. "I know there's a half dozen cookies missing from that plate."

"So much for a nap before dinner." Harper yawned, "I thought they were for us and they are very good. How much do you get for a plate that size?" He was pulling his wallet out of his back pocket. "Here's a ten will that cover it? You won't even have to take them out of the house. Consider they're paid for."

She placed the box on the table. A cut out doily was visible through the clear view top. "I declare, Harper, your sweet tooth is going to be the life of you, yet." He reached over to pull her onto his lap.

"Have you heard from Haley this week?" Harper's thought traveled back to when their lives seemed normal, a son and a daughter, their pride and joy. It still hurt. He'd lost his son, Grant Harper Gipson; he let the name roll silently in his memory, Haley's brother. The ghost that lived with them reared up to scream, "And Haley went to prison." Emotion slapped him in the face. "We've had some good times, some bad," His voice was low, raspy. "Sometimes we have to eat a plate of cookies to feel better."

"I know," she whispered, "Sometimes it seems more bad than good, except God brought us through." Their lawyer at the time called it a conspiracy. Because Haley was dating Race and the police were hunting him, they used Haley to draw him out, except it didn't work. Dorothy still wondered if there was a body in the casket when they attended his funeral. Word had circulated that Race was out of the country living high. "There would be no other way," she said, not realizing she spoke out loud.

"What did you say, Hon?"

Dorothy gave an embarrassed laugh and got off his lap. "Do you think we're too old for me to sit on your lap?" She stooped to kiss him. "I love you."

"If we get too old to love each other we just as well call it quits," Harper replied. He drew a deep breath. "Why don't we go somewhere, I'm feeling a bit down. Maybe it's the weather, whatever it is I can't get much lower." The house phone rang and he looked to Dorothy. "You want to get that or let it go?"

"Gipson residence." Dorothy laughed. "How was I to know it was you?" She was walking back to Harper. "It's your adopted son."

"I feel better, already. What's going on?" He listened to Andrew. "By golly, we will. It's Friday night and none of the crews are working tomorrow, we'll see you in about twenty minutes." He was smiling.

"Andrew said we hadn't been over to play with the kids and if we are going to be honorary grandparents we need to fulfill the responsibility. Spoken like a lawyer, right?" His grin kept spreading. "That boyo has turned out even better than I hoped." Harper was rubbing his hands together. "They want us to come for dinner. Ain't that something, we delivered him from a jail cell and he became a lawyer. You can't beat that."

* * * * * *

Harper patted his stomach. "Anne that was absolutely the best pasta dish I've ever eaten. What do you call it?"

"If I'm thinking right Bitty called it taco lasagna and she always insisted we had to have a garden salad with cranberries and garlic croutons to go with the dish." Anne shook her head, remembering Bitty. "I loved Bitty. When I was low funded and Ellen took me in, you might as well say Bitty did too. She ran that house with such skill. When we came home evenings from school, dinner was ready. If we had a tear in a garment, Bitty mended it. Oh, how we appreciated her. Ruthie had the best sitter ever."

"And how's your doctor and his wife? They are considered the real grandparents, aren't they?"

Anne flushed with pleasure. She reached over to touch Dorothy's hand. "Just like you two." They…"

Andrew interrupted. "Would you believe Dr. Lonzo and little Momma want to adopt Anne?"

"They don't have children, do they?"

Anne shook her head. "They don't have anyone. They love Andy and now Addy, too. Andy's the one couldn't call her by her name, I was Momma, so she became little Momma. You know she's probably not five feet tall. They are insistent, Dorothy, I've held off two years listening to their weekly adoption plan." Anne almost giggled. "I can't help but be honored they would even ask. They are such loving people."

"Do you have a living relative, Anne?"

"My mother is alive, as far as I know but she was never around when I was a kid. I lived with my uncle."

"So you are estranged, any hope of getting back together as a family?"

"My mother doesn't know where I am or anything about my life. She never cared. On that, I guess not."

Andrew had been listening. "Come on, girls, we are getting a little melancholy. Let me show you the studio that is supposed to be my office but twenty plus aged young man gets it first. Did you say Jacob, Anne?" He turned to Dorothy, "And remember Dorothy, Anne and Andy have Harriet."

"I think he feels just a little threatened," Anne explained, "But he's the one held his hand up and told Brother Joe we would love to room one of the people on the list and Brother Joe chose who it would be. So come next week, we meet Jacob." She grinned, "And on the other subject, you know Harriet loves us."

"I'm sure it will be just fine. Boyo, if you didn't choose yourself, then that means God's sending who he wants you to keep." He put a firm hand on Andrew's bicep and gave him a shake. "Wait and see. God's in charge."

"Well, you and Dorothy took me in and that was a turning point in my life. I appreciate you both."

Dorothy felt relief. Harper had put the sadness behind them. With Andrew he always made an effort, because Andrew was the one he pulled out of despair the night little Andy was hit by the car and nearly died. Still, she couldn't help but wonder why Haley hadn't called. Andrew was opening the door to the room where their visitor, Jacob would stay.

"It has a refrigerator, a microwave, just a little kitchenette, mind you," Andrew was saying. "Here's the bathroom, and it's a good thing we put in the shower for when I return from golf." He gave Anne a dubious look. "Except I'm sorry to say I won't be using it."

"I didn't know you played golf, Andrew. When do you have time?" Dorothy leaned forward, waiting for his answer.

"I don't," Andrew was laughing. "And now don't look like I'd have a shower to use if I did."

"For heaven's sakes, Andrew," Anne poked him in the ribs. "I've got to run check on the babies."

* * * * * *

Anne returned. "They're sound asleep. Addy's on her stomach, little behind up in the air snoozin' away and you know I wondered if Andy would be jealous and not want to share, but he loves her and there's no problem."

"Your children are both sweet natured." Dorothy glanced across at Harper. "Maybe Haley will give us a grandbaby to go along with Andy and Addy and thinking on the babies being asleep, we need to go."

"Yes, we do. See you at church Sunday, Boyo." He hugged Andrew and kissed Anne on the cheek. "Besides that, our Haley hasn't checked in. I don't know about her Momma but I'm wondering why not."

They were in the car when Harper said, "Fine young people, aren't they, Momma. Imagine Anne taking in Andrew's love child when he put her through hell." He drew a deep breath. "I tell you I ate too much of that wonderful dish." He glanced Dorothy's way, "You are quiet. You worried or do you know something I don't know? Are you trying to think it's her new job?"

"No. I don't. I was just thinking how Andrew turned his life around and he and his mother reconciled a year or two ago, but she went back to Tennessee and yes, it could be Haley's new job."

"All right then, I'll try not to worry. Has Andrew told his mother about Addy?"

"I didn't ask, but they are blessed to have the Lonzo's so crazy over them and Harriet, too."

"Which brings us to Marigold; you've not mentioned Marigold and Matt lately, nor Ellen and Dan."

"Life gets busy, Harper. I think we're all tired. That's why I didn't suggest taking anyone in as the Gates and the Graves. I didn't feel I could take care of them. Could you, working the hours you do?"

"No, not right now, though we're so blessed and those poor people can't help their homes were flooded." He peered at the clock. "What time is it?"

"It's nine thirty. Not too late to call Haley." She smiled in the darkness. "Isn't that what you're thinking?"

CHAPTER 3

TWINS

"**O**kay, Daddy of the year. It's time you cast your bread upon the waters and see if it returns to you?"

Daniel awoke Saturday morning to find Ellen already dressed, a twin, hanging over her arm like a wet noodle; Holly and Noel were still in their pj's and their jammie bottoms were puffed up like marshmallows. "Oh, no, they're waterlogged," he reached for Noel but Noel clung to Ellen and Holly fell into his arms. "How're you baby bumpkin?" Holly's little hands patted each side of his face, until she dipped down and put her mouth on his chin. "You given me sugars, baby bumpkin?" Ellen changed Noel and now he was crawling across Daniel's stomach.

"Here you go Mommie; this one's going to start spoutin like a fountain if you don't change her."

Noel sit up straight then fell back on Daniel. Ellen heard their heads meet. "Hey, Buddy, you just cracked our skulls." Daniel was rubbing a red spot on his forehead while Noel was scrubbing away at the back of his head. "Boy, you are tough," Daniel pulled him into the crook of his arm. "Shut the doors good, Mommie, so they don't get out of this room if I drift off, and the door to the bathroom."

Ellen looked around the room. "Floor's clean, except for one pair of shoes; everything else is up off the floor. They'll crawl around, pull up on things, but don't worry when they want you they'll stand and slap the bed or pull til the cover comes off you." She leaned across to kiss him. "But Daddy of the year, you won't sleep. I promise you that but I won't tell you why." She gave him another smack on the lips and he pulled her down beside him.

"You could stay home and we'd just buy a few dozen cookies to help the ladies out. What do you think?"

Laughing, Ellen rolled off the bed, straightened her clothes and headed for the door. "I promised to help." She threw the twins a kiss. "Ruthie has Danny and Sammy in her room. They're good with her."

The twins were standing at the foot of the bed staring at him. "Mommy's going to sell cookies."

"Blah Blah Blah Blah Blah…." The twins began their blahing, changing key every few minutes, heads together, arms on each other's shoulders, Daniel could only watch. Whatever they were saying they seemed to understand each other. If one crawled around the floor, the other did. If one slapped the bed covers the other joined in. It was the blah blah, he heard loud and clear and it never stopped until they tired their selves out and lay on the floor, face to face with one of Ellen's shoes in their arms. Ellen's robe lay across the chair arms. Daniel covered them. They would sleep an hour.

He made the bed, tiptoed down the hall to listen to Ruthie reading to the boys. It came to him. Ruthie was three when he and Ellen married, now they were a family of seven; perfect number. He smiled all the way back to his and Ellen's room, checked on the babies who were still sleeping and closed the door. He had just enough time to restudy the lesson for Sunday. After commitment Sunday he had accepted the nine year old boy's class. They gave him a run for his money. Yeah, he thought I let them sucker me into that one. If they ask a question from the Bible he couldn't answer he had to put a dollar in the jar but it was all right, it kept the boys searching for answers. They learned a lot together.

He was putting his Bible and study book away to check on the twins when the phone rang. It was Matt. "Hang on a minute, Matt, I'm checking on the twins." He left the door slightly open to hear when they awoke and settled back down in the recliner, a direct line of view to where they slept. "They're still sleeping. How is it at your house while the Mommies' sell cookies?" He smiled at Matt's reply. "How's life treating you, that other incident smoothing out?"

Matt had been the center of a woman's attention, other than his wife. When she married Andrew's partner everyone hoped the matter was settled but Britany James wasn't one to be concerned with what others hoped. Now as Daniel listened, there were no incidents but Britany was due to deliver her baby any day. "Well, we're praying for you, Matt. One woman in our life is enough." They both laughed.

They ended their conversation saying they would see each other on Sunday at Christ Church. Following church the group enjoyed dinner together at one of the three restaurants that served macaroni and cheese and they all agreed life had changed, that item on the menu allowed them a few moments peace to eat their own lunch. All had young children except Harriet had none and Dorothy and Harper had Haley, newly married in a new career.

* * * * * *

HALEY

Pulling the skirt down another inch, Haley was ready to show the house on Brighton Circle. She had passed the test and was now a full fledged member of Dalton Realtors, but she had to prove she could "mustor" as the Senior Dalton said, which his son explained meant last through the most grueling week she could imagine. "Sell three houses in one week and I'll say your worth hiring, well, so you say we already hired you, all right then sell three and we'll keep you on and remember it's not all selling and making money, you have to take a day answering the phone like the rest of the gals."

"Don't mind him," the son said, "he's trying to see what you're made of. He'll either make you or break you and I know you won't believe this but he may even become your best friend."

She remembered his advice as she dressed the next morning. "Always look your best," he said. "If your customer wants to wear flipflops and a bad quoted T shirt, let 'em. You will make that house look good. If they make cracks about a house you know is three times better than the one they live in, that's all right, too. Just smile. Don't ever agree or bring down the property you're selling. The next person doesn't need to hear that." He pat her shoulder and said, "Good luck, kid."

Pulling on the skirt again to make it an inch longer she realized if she stayed in this business the "teenage styles" as he called them were a thing of the past. She didn't have to dress matronly but she did need class. She'd done away with the mass of curly hair, straightened it into a shoulder length page boy, put on her horn rimmed glasses and resembled something half way between a school marm and a ticket seller at the airport.

She left Jeremy sitting at the breakfast table and met his dad on the way out. He stopped to admire her, "Hey, now, you look good young lady." Jonathan Southern paused on the steps. "Where you headed so early?"

"I'm showing a house at the Cape on Brighton Circle. It's high dollar, you may know number one twelve. Wish me luck." He was shaking his head. Everyone knew Brighton was where the wealthy lived.

"I've heard the early bird gets the worm," they said, together.

Laughing, she got in the car for the hour and a half drive to the Cape. "Does this happen often," she'd asked the elderly Dalton, "getting houses to sell in other towns more than an hour away?"

"We take them if they're large enough, honey, that means more money for you and me both."

The clients arrived, two men and a woman, she walked through with them, explaining the various features, things she didn't know existed and had never thought to own, they were not overly impressed and hard to read as to whether they were interested or not. She was back at the office by one thirty. The elderly Dalton asked, "How did it go?"

"I'm not sure," she replied. "These people are hard to read; they make very few comments."

He began to laugh. "Would you believe they want to walk through again? He's ready to buy, but she thinks there may be a better place down the road."

"Did you look at my schedule and make an appointment for next week?"

"No, I made it for six tonight. They are going out of country tomorrow evening and want to make a decision, one way or the other. They want all lights on and access to all things mechanical."

Haley thought about Jeremy asking her to be home early and now she needed to stay over. She called but missed him and left a message.

* * * * * *

JONATHAN SOUTHERN

He began drinking as soon as he arrived home. It was one of those days he'd dealt with the hard-nosed district manager. Who was he to tell Jon Southern 'you have to update' when he had never owned a thing in his life. He had worked his way up in the company, pandered after the family that began it all. His son married up, but Vince Galooly remained the same snot nosed boy he'd attended River High with.

"You've heard what corporate wants, take down your fancy southern columns and get their colors going. Your competitors are heeding my advice which comes straight from the top. Now get it done or you are out."

Jonathan had spent a fortune making his dealership the lead of the south. They wanted him to rip out a million dollars' worth of style for glass fronted tiles in their colors? What did it matter what the exterior looked like if the dealership met and surpassed its quota and had become number one seller in the field?

In two hours he had passed from melancholy to a temperament of hostility. When Katherine asked, "Don't you think you've drank enough? How about putting it away and let's go out to dinner?"

"Go by yourself," he replied. Surly and uncaring he gave her a smirking glance and filled his glass again.

"Please, Jonathan, Jeremy and Haley are supposed to stop by but we could invite them to join us."

"I'm not hungry." He hadn't meant to scream. She took offense, as always, tears brightened her eyes.

"You are killing our marriage," she said.

"You want out?" He sneered, staggering to his feet, waving the bottle in one hand, the glass dripping from his hand. "You think you will find another bozo to supply your money?" He lurched toward her.

"Frankly, the bozo I'm with leaves me so discouraged I spend very little money."

Close enough to touch, he reached out, the glass in his thumb and forefinger and let the others rest on her shoulder. "Nice pearls you have on Kathryn, did I buy those little treasures for you?"

"You did." She shrank away. "They mean a lot to me, Jonathan. That was in a day when you were a gentleman and knew how to handle your drink."

Dropping the glass, he grabbed at the pearls pulling tight until her hands went up in protection as her throat reddened. "Please, Jonathan, don't do this."

"I figure they're mine. My money bought them, if I want to dress the façade I will and if I want to destroy it, it's my right. Neither you or corporate can tell me what to do." With that he gave a yank and the pearls scattered down Kathryn's body, rolling across the floor. "You want to go eat out and show the world who you are, let's go." He was half dragging her across the room. She managed to skewer her purse and lock the door behind them. He was past the stage of reasoning.

"Let me drive," she pleaded. Breaking loose, she scooted behind the wheel and waited for him to get in on the passenger side. "Promise me you won't make a scene. It would go against who the people of this town think you are, the great Jonathan Southern."

Smirking again, he tilt his head a crazy angle and stared at her through insolent eyes. "I hear you, can't have the people thinking

I have even one problem, which would be your ridiculous old fashioned ways." He lay back, seeming to enjoy the ride until she drove in to their favorite eating place. "Same old, same old," he quipped, "boring and old, just like you." Nevertheless, they followed the maitre d' to their table. "How many of this town's good old boys are seated by the maître d'?" He gave his patronizing laugh. "You remind me of an old hen ready to flog me."

"At this point, Jonathan, if I could, I would."

"Is that so?" His words ran together. "I tell you what, then, I'll just go and you have yourself a nice dinner." He left her sitting there as the waiter lurked around the corner wondering what to do.

Kathryn waited and then went outside to locate their car. It was gone and so was Jonathan. Now she began to worry with him drunk and driving.

Jonathan put all the previous happenings out of his mind. Something kept reminding him of a Brighton address. He was past due. He was supposed to be there at One Twelve Brighton and he was late. The traffic swerved around him driving faster than the speed limit allowed but he had to keep up with them and pressed his foot down hard on the gas pedal.

Most of the lights were off in the building but the main door was open. He slipped inside, seeing a light in the distance and began making his way toward it. A woman's shadow slipped back and forth, how had Kathryn arrived before him? So she felt animosity toward him, did she? Time to teach Kathryn a lesson which was exactly what he intended to do.

* * * * * *

It was a grueling hour. The couple had brought their own electrician. The man never sought her advice on any piece of equipment. A probe here, some kind of hand sized tool, he pecked on this, undone screws on that, said uh huh and hmmm a lot until she thought she couldn't stand on her feet another minute. Just when she decided to tell the couple she would have to pick up where they left off today, tomorrow, the two men went into a huddle and the client said, "We'll take it."

"We will be in your office bright and early tomorrow morning," the man said. The two climbed into a truck with the electrician and were gone as quick as she could scan the empty lot of not one vehicle beside hers.

She had to lock all doors and turn out the lights and there was one panel the electrician removed and forgot to go back to replace. She stepped out of the high heels, removed her jacket and retraced her way through the rooms flipping light switches. If she hurried she wouldn't need the flash light. Disgusted she remembered it was in her jacket pocket. A miniature it gave excellent light. She was concentrating on the panel putting screws in with a paring knife by the light from the hall when she heard a noise. Now footsteps, were coming on, loitering at first, and then moving faster. Hadn't she locked the doors? She listened, the sound was not high heels, it was the slap of a man's leather sole shoe on the floor. The hall light went out.

Her mind was on alert, something really wasn't right. Her body was going numb with fear. Lord. Lord, don't let anything happen to me. She couldn't see her hand in front of her face. She made up her mind to call out when suddenly arms were around her; from behind someone had his chin resting on her head, the smell of liquor was on his breath, kissing her cheek his head bent, nuzzling all the while holding her secure. "Please. Please don't do this."

Haley threw her arms out, trying to lessen his hold. He chuckled as if it were a game. "Be still," he said. She raised her foot trying to stomp his. Buckling her body, she loosened his hands, as she slid downward, all fours on the floor trying to gain purchase. Pushing away, when he grabbed the top she wore, little more than a camisole, she heard the fabric rip and it was only a moment until his hands were tearing away any remaining clothing. There was no reasoning with him. He was seriously drunk. "Please God, please, don't let this happen." Whoever he was, he did not hear nor care she spoke.

Giving one last effort she leaned forward then snapped back with all she possessed, his head bounced as her own cracked skulls, his arms around her loosened and she landed on the floor, her cheek sliding on the rough tile. Anger roared through his veins as he found her and backhanded her. Haley felt her head spin. Would he break her neck? Pain shot down her spine, radiated to her eyes, blackness was claiming her as she fought to stay conscious. Blood ran down the side of her face. She swiped it away. For a moment she recognized a familiar smell…what was it? His cologne or aftershave, she wasn't certain. She was crying, the cry more a moan of grief…but no one heard.

Now she was storing what she must remember. He was tall, not heavy, age she couldn't decide. He wore a bracelet on his left arm. That too, was familiar, but her senses were sliding away, nothing was clear. You know who this is, her mind screamed and she screamed back, who is it? I don't. I don't. I don't." She had given her best trying to ward off the inevitable, the darkness claimed her and she was glad.

* * * * * *

Before an hour was up, he had done what he felt must be done. Leaving by the same door, Jonathan slipped out into the night. Kathryn had become like Corporate; she had no right to talk down to him. This would teach her not to flaunt her ways before him. If she was upset over the pearls he bought them, he had rights. He was feeling the alcohol making him sleepy and ready to sleep now, not after another hour on the interstate with crazy drivers. He drove down to the river, parked the car and locked the doors. Laying the seat back as far as it would go, Jonathan slept. Jeremy found him there the next morning. He didn't ask who drove Jeremy to the Cape, he supposed it was Haley. He liked the girl; she was devoted to his son. Going home he found no such devotion. Kathryn was gone.

* * * * * *

Haley awakened, alone, unaware of time, on the floor, a heap of misery; it was a bad dream, except her clothes were destroyed, and lying in rags around her. Her abductor was gone. It was the hour of first daylight she guessed as she drug herself up, surveying any damage to the house. In frenzy using the torn blouse she wiped the floor, righted the rug and put on the jacket. She had to get out of there. What if he came back? She remembered then, what the man, her client said, "We will be back first thing tomorrow morning." She called the older Dalton. Hearing his voice brought such comfort she burst into tears.

"Are you crying?" he asked.

"Yes, will you promise to keep what I tell you between us?"

"I will." Alarmed he asked, "What happened?" Fearing the worst, he pursued "was it our client?"

When she finished telling him, "Do I need to come for you?" She said no. "Go home," he said, "or to a motel. I will meet with your people and you will receive full credit."

Haley called the hospital and was connected to the Emergency Room. Based on their information she was not ready to file a report. She drove to the nearest motel and got a room. In the safety of the room she cried for what was lost; her trust of people was beaten down, all she could do now was pray what happened had no effect on her marriage. She sobbed into the pillow to lessen the terrible moans that came from her as independently as if she were not present. She needed a human voice to comfort and tell her life would be all right in the months to come but she knew she would never forget what happened. She could not call her parents; they could not stand the blow of their daughter hurting.

Weak, unable to go on, she tried to call Ellen and Marigold. It was hard to believe the world outside was going on as natural as the day before. Oh, Lord, she prayed please send someone to me. Please. She had missed her parent's weekly visit. She cried even harder, trying once more to reach Marigold or Ellen.

* * * * * *

JEWEL

Jewel arrived as planned on Monday. She was a slender young woman, fair skinned with a few freckles, dressed in a button front blouse and a gathered skirt, something few saw these days. Ellen and Ruthie showed her the room she would stay in and she was immensely pleased. "We are trying to replace our home with proper bedding," she said, "and just about everything else. This is a pretty room."

* * * * * * *

It was Tuesday and Daniel came home early to help Ellen but Ruthie met him instead. "Where's Mommie?"

"Daddy, she left after getting a call but there's a note for you in the ice compartment of the frig."

"Well that's intriguing. I've never had a note from the refrigerator before. I'm excited."

Ruthie grinned. "Daddy, you are teasing me."

"So what's going on here? Where are the twins?"

"Did you forget? Jewel is here. She has both sets of twins in the family room. She's teaching Samuel and Daniel their numbers and Holly and Noel think they are learning too."

"Is she a teacher?" Dan tilt his head just so, studying Ruthie. "Wasn't that your job? You didn't have to give it up."

"Jewel said she began college and then the flood hit her parent's home and washed away everything of value and she thought it selfish for her to go back when they needed the money elsewhere." Dan kissed her on the top of her hair. "I don't mind if Jewel works with the twins. I have other things to do."

"You're sure?" She was smiling as she nodded yes. "You are the best daughter a daddy could ever imagine." Ruthie beamed. "So, Mommy left in a hurry." Daniel questioned but if Ruthie knew why she wasn't saying.

The hour grew late, Daniel had read the note that said if it became six o clock and she had not returned to sit the food out of the oven, feed everyone and give the twins baths. There was a lipstick kiss over the last words, "I know you will enjoy the bath's Daddy of the year. They are most energizing."

There was a conversation lull at the dinner table; Dan was worried since Ellen had not called. Even the twins were subdued, their eyes on Jewel. "How did the lesson on numbers go, Jewel?" Daniel was trying to be hospitable but the effort was weak.

"Fine, Mr. Gates. They are lovely smart children."

"Sometimes mischievous, too," he replied. "You'll have to watch out for Samuel. He's a character."

"Thank you for the opportunity to be around them. I hope one day to finish my education and teach."

"Are there no young children in your family, Jewel?" He thought a moment and finished, "And you have no plans to marry soon?" He grinned. "I'm teasing you, now, Jewel but you can answer if you wish."

Jewel's cheeks grew a bit rosy. "No, Sir, there are no children and for that matter no young men in my area." She saw the question in his eyes. "My parents are older, Sir. We don't get out much."

"How have you managed your education?"

"There's a Community College in the next town. I did the first two years there, and then stayed with my daddy's sister for the next year at University but I was home when the flood came and wiped my momma and daddy's home off the face of the earth and we're just lucky we are alive." She was quiet a moment as if considering whether to continue. "My daddy didn't believe in banks, Sir. Our savings went with the house. The house and farm were paid for but who will fund a man without possession to back it up?"

"Please forgive my questions, Jewel." Daniel's expression was troubled. "We are so fortunate to have everything within reach. But there are young men..."

"No, Sir," Jewel interrupted, "I am a very plain person and my wardrobe would not appeal to anyone."

Ruthie stepped to where Jewel was sitting and held out her hand. "Come with me, Jewel. The garden Daddy Daniel has created for Momma is beautiful any time of the year. I want you to see something."

They slipped on jackets and went out the back door. "You see, Jewel, the crocus are blooming and the hyacinth and the daffodils are headed that way. Did your mother have a flower garden?" Ruthie led her to the large angel with extended wings. Raising the top of the bench she took out Ellen's Bible, closed the top and motioned for Jewel to sit beside her. "I know you attend church. Is it considered a country church?" In her mind, Ruthie saw the white board church with its tall steeple raised to the heavens.

"Why, yes, it is. How did you know?" Jewel squeezed her hand. "It is most important to our people."

"And Thomas Sterling, Jewel, why is he the one you think of, Thomas Sterling will not apply himself."

"I thought perhaps I loved him," she replied, "But then again, maybe that is because he and his cousin Benny are the only two available." She smiled sweetly. "Now that I'm here I have hope."

"That's good." Ruthie was turning in the big Bible to Jeremiah 29:11. Do you remember Jeremiah 29:11, Jewel? In my spirit I feel God has a special reason for you coming to the Cape. Do you?" She waited but Jewel didn't reply. "This is what the scripture says. "For I know the plans I have for you declares the Lord. "Plans to prosper you and not to harm you, plans to give you hope and a future." Ruthie closed the Bible. "I felt like you needed the scripture, Jewel; for encouragement, and I know God is going to bless you here with us."

Tears sprang in Jewel's eyes. "I surely needed to hear that, Ruthie. Thank you." Her soft voice was barely more than a whisper. "Ruthie, how did you know about Thomas Sterling?" She was quiet, thinking. "I don't remember telling you anything about HIM; I try not to let anyone know."

Ruthie was giggling. "Come on, there's a swing back here and don't worry, you are going to meet someone else. I was sitting in church when I first saw him in my mind and I had no idea who he was."

The fountain was running as the sky turned black of night with stars twinkling in God's heaven. "Ruthie," Jewel was swinging through the air, her feet straight in front of her, "How old are you?

I'm almost twenty four and I like being with you, you seem to fit in with any age and that is a gift."

Ruthie smiled, her mind had journeyed away for a second; she knew inside the house Daddy Daniel was worrying over Momma as he gave the boys a bath. She would give Noel and Holly baths, but her thoughts strayed to a girl huddled on a bed, crying. She heard Momma's voice and Marigold was there.

"Jewel, do you mind if we go in, I think Daddy is worried over Momma."

"It's getting cool, anyway, Ruthie." Jewel watched Ruthie lead the way through the garden. "I've never seen a garden like this. It seems the stars in the sky shine brighter and nowhere else have I seen the Easter lilies bloom but it is almost Easter and you…Ruthie are you really only seven years old?"

Laughing, Ruthie skipped down the path, "My Momma says, sometimes age doesn't matter?"

"I seldom talk to people, Ruthie, but with you it's easy."

'Why, Jewel?" Ruthie glanced back, Jewel didn't answer and she wondered why.

* * * * * *

MARIGOLD

They both were in shock; Marigold received the call and was to contact Ellen. "What shall we do?"

"We have to go. First I must see if Jewel and Ruthie can sit with the twins until Dan comes home."

"Matt's home early but my vans low on gas. Can you pick me up?"

Marigold came out as soon as she entered the drive. "She's called again, there's something wrong."

"We'll know shortly." Ellen replied. "Times like this you don't know what to expect."

In their wildest dreams they would not have thought of Haley sitting on the bed, her body bruised and aching, her beautiful skin blotched and two good sized lumps, one below her left eye the other above her right. Ellen touched her forehead and she jerked nearly screaming out loud.

"How did this happen?" Fresh tears rolled down Haley's cheeks as she tucked her chin to her chest and refused to look up at them. "Do you need to go to the doctor, is anything broken?"

Haley shuddered as though to avoid entrance to her thoughts, "I went", she lied. "I'm fine."

"Do you need to tell your parents?"

A frantic look came into Haley's eyes. "No, don't tell them. It would break their hearts."

"What can we do?" She and Marigold were on their knees in front of Haley, now, and as she burst into tears again, Marigold reached and pulled her into her arms. "Haley, has someone raped you?"

It was the moan of a wounded animal that could not understand why someone hurt her. She began to rock back and forth; back and forth and finally she nodded. Ellen and Marigold drew deep breaths.

"Our worst fear," Marigold whispered.

"Why are you here?" Ellen rose to sit on the bed by Haley. "Why won't you let us take you to your parents'? You need their care." Ellen put her arms around the two, her head on Haley's shoulder, "Or, do you want to go to your home, Haley, to Jeremy."

"Noooo." She began to explain, great heaves between each word. "I left him a voice mail that I had an early appointment in the morning and I was staying over." The sobs increased to the point Ellen was afraid someone would hear in the hall and turn them in. "He can't see me like this. I have to have time."

"But how did you explain this if you went to the doctor?"

"I told them I was alone and fell down an incline and rolled and there were huge rocks."

"And why would you have done that?" Marigold was intrigued by Haley's answer.

"I am in real estate now," Haley managed, with a sob. "I passed the test." She was wailing, "It was supposed to be a good thing, a celebration and look what happened."

"Come go home with me, Haley," Marigold centered herself, taking both of Haley's hands, making Haley look at her. "Matt's there, but he would never tell anyone and you know you need to be with someone." Rising, Marigold found Haley's suitcase and began rounding up the stray items from around the room. "I can't stay with you because of my children but you can stay as long as you wish in our home. Now, slip your shoes on."

"You are sure you don't need to go to the hospital and you don't wish to share anything else with us?" Ellen asked, mindful of the seriousness of the situation, knowing if Haley chose not to talk or share there was nothing they could do.

"Thank you," Haley whispered. "It is too painful. If I'm to keep my marriage I must remain silent."

It was almost eleven by the time Ellen dropped Marigold and Haley at the Langley home. "I'm sorry," Haley whispered. "I will make it up to you, Ellen. I promise. Thank you for coming."

"You don't owe me anything, Haley. I love you and I want what's best for you. Please call Jeremy and tell him you are all right. He will be worried sick."

"I will." Haley hugged Ellen, "but it won't be easy, Ellen. Jeremy will fill hurt."

* * * * * *

Daniel met her at the door. "Oh, Babe, I was getting so worried. Are you all right?"

"Is everyone in bed?" She asked quietly, waiting for his answer and when he nodded, she sighed in relief. "What I tell you has to remain between us, Dan." He nodded again. "It was Haley needed us. She called Marigold and ask us to come. The words are never easy for a woman; she was raped earlier today but that's not all, in his wrath he beat her. She is pretty bruised and a knot over one eye and under the other which in truth, eventually, what's on the outside will go away."

"Jeremy?"

"No, I don't think so, but she wouldn't go home. She's at Marigolds."

"You are so weary," Daniel took her hand and led her to the bedroom, piece by piece he undressed her of clothing. "Do you need to shower?" She nodded. He turned the water on, waiting until it was warm. Ellen stepped in and stood there letting the stream wash away the filth she had felt since Haley's admission she had been raped. Slowly, as Daniel waited, she begin to feel the cleansing.

He wrapped the towel around her using a second to dry her hair and when it was time slipped the gown over her head and helped her into bed. "This worries me when you tire this way."

At the Langley household, Matt was asleep with M.J. in the curve of one arm. Marigold checked their daughter, snuggled in a little round ball, pacifier in her mouth sleeping soundly. Saying a silent prayer of thanksgiving, she gathered her night clothes and went to the bathroom where Haley had finished. "I'm sleeping here, with you," she whispered, "no need waking the house this late, is there?"

"Thank you, Marigold; I didn't want to be alone tonight, too many thoughts reliving themselves in my head." The misery of the day had etched itself into her features. "I can't tell you, it's as though I'm walking and talking in someone else's body. You never think it will happen to you."

"I can't imagine," Marigold replied. "I'm going to take a quick rinse." When she returned, Haley was still awake, her cheeks damp with tears. But she pat the empty side of the bed and tried to smile. Marigold stooped and kissed her brow, tucked the cover around her and went to the other side and slid in bed. "If you need anything wake me, if you want to talk, whatever you need I'm here for you. Okay?"

Fresh tears spilled from Haley's eyes. "I'll make it now." Marigold pulled her friend close and held her. "You have been here, Marigold, in this place of despair and not understanding why, haven't you?"

And so, in the next days a story was concocted between the three, hesitant at first but not knowing any other way to tell Jeremy so he wouldn't worry and in time Haley's parents would be told the same. While showing property in the Cape, the interested party left and Haley got her heel caught and took a spill which left her bruised and the lumps on her face. If at all possible, they would not mention the three being together that night. Few details missed their consideration.

* * * * * *

Ruthie heard her mother return home. Something was bothering her. While in the garden *in her mind* she had *seen* Haley sitting on a bed in a room that reminded her of a hotel and she heard her mother and Marigold whispering but she did not see them. What she saw left her concerned for Haley and afraid of the man shaking Haley and slapping her. Haley was fighting to be free. Ruthie wanted to tell her mother but Ruthie knew the exhaustion that comes from experiencing violence. She waited.

Mid evening the next day, while the twins napped, Ruthie asked Jewel, "Would you watch the babies, all four, while I walk Momma in her garden? She doesn't seem to feel good today and the garden always refreshes her." Finding Ellen, Ruthie said, "Come on, you haven't seen the little tulips blooming in the garden. Let's wear a sweater because it's cool."

* * * * * *

"Oh, they are sweet," Ellen exclaimed. "Thank you for showing me, Ruthie." Ellen gave her a hug.

"Momma, look at this picture." Ellen took it and her body stiffened a bit as she handed it back.

"Why would you show me a picture of Haley's wedding?"

"Momma, that's the man I saw hurting Haley. I think you know who he is."

"Wait, you know?" Ellen sank onto the bench beneath the big angel. "Oh, Ruthie, I'm so sorry." Her child was too young to have to know the baser make up of a man, but God had given Ruthie understanding. In the world, there will always be problems, Ellen thought holding her child, we never know who is next.

CHAPTER 4

Anne collected her children after work as one did a rare coin, except there were two now and Harriet insisted she and Hattie could care for Addy and Andy as well as Harriet's very own grandchildren, M.J. and Maggie. The two were delighted to dress Maggie and Addy in the clothes Harriet bought and to send them home looking like little princess. More and more they were bringing in Hattie's granddaughter to help with household chores. Marigold laughed about the buildup of toys in the toy room, remembering there was a time Harriet had not understood how easily that could happen.

Marigold came by as Anne prepared to leave. "There were two ladies in the shop that attend Christ Church and they were speaking about the arrival of the ones staying in homes that had lost their possessions and I happened to wonder if yours arrived, Anne."

"Yes, his name is Evan Jacobs." She laughed, "At first we thought his name was Jacob. Anyway, he's in his late twenties, evidently plays a guitar as he has one." Thinking she pursed her lips and tilt her head, "I guess that's about it, he's quiet and he seems, much to Andrew's dismay to really like the office-slash-studio that offers him privacy rather than being in the house with us."

"Well, if you don't have children and then all of a sudden you are living in close quarters with them it might be a challenge, don't you think? So, do you feed him or is he on his own?

"We have dinner together every night, otherwise with both of us working; I doubt we'd ever see him. We did stock the frig with enough to keep him from starving each meal."

"Will you be bringing him to Friday nights gathering at church?"

"Isn't that what it's for, for the church body to be acquainted?"

"Ellen's the one told me about it," Marigold replied. "It sounds interesting. I think we'll be going. Speaking of going, I need to get on the road or Matt will be home before me and start calling."

"Are you working on someone's home presently?"

"No, but I have a call on my phone someone that's interested asked me to stop by." She checked her phone. "Where is 201 Greenwich? Doesn't that sound familiar?"

Anne asked, "Isn't that on Ellen's street? They're 200, being on the end, aren't they?"

"I've not been there since Christmas dinner but it seems they did mention a new builder." She glanced toward the toy room. "Honesty, what's keeping them? I called. Harriet was going to bring the kids. Let's see what's going on. They are usually putting toys away."

"We've not seen this before," Anne remarked. Hattie and Harriet were down on their knees crawling through the tent just as the children. "Hey, you older two, we need your assistance. Do you need ours?"

Harriet tried to rise. "I got down here but getting up is a different story. I'll crawl over to the sofa?" That was failure, too. "Oh, my goodness, call the tow truck, I can't get out of the floor." Hattie was in the same shape. The two began to laugh at their own predicament. "I never thought it would come to this." The children gathered around Harriet. "Nanny's hurt," they said. "No, Nanny can't get up," Harriet explained.

Marigold whispered to Anne, "She would be my mother." Shaking her head, she held out a hand. "Come, on, I'll help you up this time but don't do that anymore." When Harriet was steady on her feet, Marigold ask, "Have you talked to Ellen? Anne thinks the people who want to see me are building by Ellen and Dan."

"I called Ellen the other night but Dan said she was with you. Where were you two? About the building, though, Dan and I talked. He says it is three sisters, not youngsters, more my age I believe."

"Hmm. Now I have to wonder what their style is."

"Well, I drove by the house and it is going to be spectacular."

"Really?" Marigold was wrapping Maggie in a blanket as Harriet buttoned M.J.'s coat. "This may be a good project; the Lord knows I need one."

"Darling, I can help you if you are in need."

"No, Mother, just once I want to make a good profit." Marigold hugged her. "We've got to go."

Anne had Addy on her hip with Andy holding her skirt tail. "I tried to call you, too, Marigold. Are you and Matt all right? Nothing going on?"

"Everything's fine." She gave a tired laugh, "unless we fall apart tonight, our schedule will be late."

Anne halted. "Something doesn't feel right, Marigold. Is it something you can't tell me?"

"Anne, Can I just say one of our mutual friends had a problem. I can't say anymore and we pray no one else figures it out, but I promised I wouldn't say anything, it could have been you answered the need that night and you would have been asked the same and we have always honored each other's request."

"That's just fine, Marigold. I don't need to know who it is but I'll pray everything goes well."

"Thank you. Prayer is exactly what is needed."

*　*　*　*　*　*

EVAN

The concourse was in festive activities when the group arrived. They had an uncanny way of all appearing around the same time. The church band was on the stage playing a medley of upbeat Christian music, loud enough to be heard but not blaring. Ellen and Dan were introducing their guest to Anne and Andrew's young man. "Jewel Chastine meet Evan Jacobs." Jewel extended a hand even as the blush rose in her face but Evan seemed not to notice. He smiled and ask her if she would like to join him at one of the tables. Anne was still holding her casserole dish but hesitant to leave. She had a question.

"I have to ask before leaving you, Evan, I know you play guitar?" He nodded. "Do you sing?"

"Yes, ma'am." He was soft spoken and Anne leaned in to say. "Would you sing for us tonight?"

"If I could use the piano, Anne, since I don't have my guitar and I'd rather not borrow one."

"I'm sure that would be fine. The band usually takes a few minutes off stage; I'll check to see if that will be a good time." She smiled and left before Evan could change his mind.

"Aren't you the bold one," Ellen teased, walking beside her. "Are you the same shy girl I once knew?"

Anne blushed now. "By coincidence, Pastor Joe was in the food section when I purchased what I needed for my dish and in passing he said there was no special music for tonight and I told him about hearing Evan." She turned serious eyes on Ellen. "He thought it would be a treat if Evan would sing."

"Good for you. Guess what? Our Jewel is trying to teach Sammy and Danny a few pre-school things and when they got out of hand the other day, she decided they needed to sing...they didn't know I was listening. That girl has a good voice. I have a feeling she was the main singer in her home church."

Back at the table, Evan asked Jewel in a very soft spoken voice, "What have I got myself into?"

She smiled wishing the sadness would leave his eyes. "The question is, what are you going to sing?"

"Any suggestions?"

"What's your range, what do you normally sing?" He hummed a little that only she could hear.

"Bridge over..."

"Yeah," he grinned now. "That's my range but not my song."

"If you play the piano, there's such a buildup in the introduction to How Great Thou Art, do you sing that?"

"I do." His fingers moved on the table top. "I don't have music; I think I can remember all of it."

"You play by note but you can play by ear?" She sat back and looked at him. "I'm impressed."

"Don't suppose you had the Flight of the Bumble Bee when you took piano?"

"How do you know I took piano?"

"I just know. You also sing." He smiled, the sadness leaving his eyes for a moment. "Let me guess. You are your parents little darling. You attend a church of reasonable attendance but there's only two or three who play the piano, and the same willing to sing Sunday morning specials but you will when called on, but you don't volunteer."

"That was a mouthful. Let me guess, you have read my diary and I'm embarrassed."

"How much of it is true."

"I am an only child. My parents had me at a later time than most. It's true I was their little darling. When you are young it's good but as you get older sometimes its embarrassing."

Did you perhaps perform the Flight of the Bumble Bee in one of your recitals, as did I?"

"I did."

"Then let's do it."

"Are you serious, on one piano?"

"Yes, and then I will do How Great Thou Art." His sad smile was confident.

"But," she practically spewed the word, "We don't know each other's style."

"Let's start out four- four- time, each *zzz* of the bumble bee let's increase until we are into it, and then let's give it a rousing run for the money. I think that will catch their attention. Are you in?" He raised his hand in a high five. She met the challenge. "Poke me in the rib when you're ready to go with it."

"I am so out of my league, in fact out of my mind. I can't believe I agreed to this. The Gates will abandon me." She took a deep breath. "I hope the band doesn't wait too long to take a break or I'll have a nervous break- down." As if they had heard, the band members were standing, stretching and leaving the stage.

Pastor Joe stepped to the microphone. "Ladies and gentlemen we are in for a treat, Evan Jacobs ..." He saw Evan pointing to Jewel. "I do believe I forgot the young ladies name, Evan."

Evan did a swan bow, very quietly saying, "I don't know your last name, Jewel." He covered by taking her hand and leading her to the piano and on the way between closed lips she said, "Chastine."

"Ladies and gentlemen, Jewel Chastine." Evan took the left side of the piano bench, Jewel the right. Evan gave the introduction, a huge build up and then as if Jewel was his student nodded his head and the four four time began. They saw the people eyeing each other as if to say, what are they doing, who said they could play for us? Jewel poked Evan in the rib and suddenly they were performing like the professionals they were. Even the youngsters playing games in the corners of the room came to watch them.

Finished, Jewel took a bow, lifted her hand gracefully to Evan and took her seat as he began. She noticed as he played the intro and moved on into the heart of the music his shoulders lifted, the tilt of his head became more pronounced as though his eyes were on a higher plain and the sadness left his countenance. In that moment she knew not what trial he had encountered but she knew music was his saving source from whatever his loss.

"You two were wonderfully entertaining," Pastor Joe remarked. "I had no idea two could play that song on one piano so effectively and Evan you blessed us with your singing. Thank you both from all of us."

Jewel had taken a vacant seat at the Gates table, thinking their time together was over, but Evan came and held out his hand waiting for her to take it. "Would you like to meet a few of our fellow refugees?"

Standing for Jewel to rise, Daniel asked, "Do you know many of the people, Evan?"

"I've met several," he replied, "but two of my neighbors are in the group; Mrs. Sanders and Mr. Tagget, sitting over there by himself. Mr. Tagget's wife was buried the week before the damn broke. It has worried him considerably whether her grave is still intact. The water was that forceful."

"I'm glad you mentioned that, Evan. Perhaps you and I could drive Mr. Tagget near the burying spot and rest his mind one way or the other. Hopefully it would be all right."

"Yes, sir." He and Jewel moved away from the table.

"Ellen, do you know if Jewel was able to contact her parents? I'm afraid I neglected to think of that."

Ruthie spoke up. "She did Daddy but the bridge is out and she couldn't go home so she came here."

"What a surprise." Marigold and Matt arrived. "Are you saving these seats for Jewel and her friend?"

"No, they are yours." Ellen opened her arms for Maggie. "Oh, look at her Sweetums, she's precious?"

"Where are Holly and Noel?"

"They have nursery and it is a welcome reprieve." Ellen was locating the older twins as she spoke.

"I just left M.J. and the twins playing on that blow up thing they brought in. See, by the hall." Marigold leaned in, her arms around Ruthie. "You said Ruthie knows; tell me, have you heard from our friend?"

"No, but Dorothy and Harper called to say they would not be here because they were going to see Haley and Jeremy. It seems Haley took a bad fall and they want to see for themselves if she is all right."

"Good. Then I can relax." She glanced at Matt. "He keeps telling me no news is good news."

"So everything is back to normal?" Ellen and Marigold exchanged *the look* as their husbands called it, meaning whatever subject they meant was fully recognized by themselves and oblivion to others. In this case it pertained to Britany James who had married Andrew's partner in the law firm.

"Nothing will ever be normal in regard to Matt's childhood friend but I'm making the effort. By the way, where are the Graves? I saw Anne with her dish and Andrew taking the children both to nursery."

Ellen laughed. "Didn't you and I do kitchen duty last time? Well, Anne and Andrew are serving tonight."

Pastor Joe was at the microphone again, "I need about four strong men to help bring two tables in from storage and a few chairs." Matt and Dan joined three others for the job. It was when they returned and Ruthie had moved on to join a group her age, Dan and Matt sat down with different expressions than when they left.

"What's wrong?"

"You know the new couple that is attending our Wednesday night group?" He shook his head, wondering if there was anything to it. "Just don't repeat me. John is his name and they are from the church Jeremy's parents attend, that's before they moved here…"

Matt continued, "John said Jeremy's parents are separated. It seems his dad is an alcoholic and went on a binge and something terrible has happened…" Matt and Daniel seemed beside themselves. "It is almost too much to repeat in our church setting; but it has set their church at odds, people take sides."

The four sit there trying to absorb the information. Ellen had hoped when Ruthie showed her the picture of Jeremy's father, what appeared to be a connection to Haley's situation was completely wrong. She had told no one. "It's not over yet," she whispered, unaware she spoke and the three heard her.

"What do you mean, Ellen?" Marigold looked to Dan for explanation when Ellen failed to reply.

"I'm clueless." Dan replied. Marigold pinned her eyes on Matt now.

"Babe, I only know what I heard and that wasn't much. We've told you."

"Ellen," Marigold came around the table to sit next to her. "If there's something we need to know, tell us. Haley is our friend and for heaven's sakes you know how protective Harper and Dorothy are of her." She was threading her fingers through her hair, nervously. "Are you thinking there will be a backlash to Jeremy and Haley…or is there more? I know there's more or I wouldn't have this horrible feeling."

"I wonder how many years Jeremy's parents have been married and now this?" Daniel asked.

"I'm going to get to the bottom of this, is that Mr. John over there by the coffee machine?"

Matt put a hand on Marigold's. "Babe, do you think you should do this, you don't know him."

"I know Haley and Jeremy," she replied and walked toward the man across the room.

"She is going to be her mother's daughter, after all," Matt said quietly. "Harriet would do the same."

For what it was worth, the three at the table felt tongue tied or perhaps they were praying for Marigold. They could see her thanking the man, shaking his hand, smiling but when she turned toward them the smile disappeared. She sat in the chair that faced Ellen now; her back was to Mr. John. "Don't look at him while I fill you in," she said. "Here's what happened. Jeremy's father, Mr. Jonathan Southern, is a very prominent equipment dealer back in Mississippi and as such he attends a number of social functions and what began as a harmless drink or two somewhere along the line became more and he is now a full-fledged alcoholic but he is also a devout church member. The other thing is, he is not a mellow drinking man when he imbibes he becomes a mean drunk. How does Mr. John know that? He and his wife lived just down the street from the Southern's and his wife befriended, was her name Kathryn? Katie? Something similar. Anyway, when he gets mean drunk, his wife says he doesn't know what he's doing and she has forgiven him for years all the while trying to get him into that twelve step program, you know to stop drinking. But this last time he didn't beat the soup out of her, the wife knows there was another woman and she thinks that woman fought to the end because Mr. Jonathan Southern was scratched up like a mad cat had hold of him, teeth bites and all, the worst part is she doesn't know what all he did to that other person but she fears the worst. She moved out because she is waiting for the other shoe to drop and some poor beat up woman come forward with a law suit against her husband."

"She believes that stuff that he doesn't know what he's doing when he's drunk?" Matt wasn't buying it. "What do you think, Dan?"

"Either he's a good liar or telling the truth." Dan shrugged and put his hands up in self-defense. "I don't know, I've never experienced any of this. Evidently the wife has been a victim for years and what she's saying is, he wakes up next morning and says, honey where did you get that black eye. Am I right?"

"Why would she move out now?" Ellen wore a puzzled expression as she looked at Marigold.

"Because it wasn't her, what if he really hurt another woman or got that one pregnant?"

"Whoa, now. We need to drop this subject," Dan said, "before someone comes along to hear us."

"We have so much to think on, right now, we don't need to go any further," Marigold agreed.

"Dan what did you think of our Jewel? She is quite shy," Ellen explained, "with us, but it seemed she and Evan hit it off pretty good. One thing for certain they are both quite accomplished on the piano."

"He's a dreamboat," Marigold offered, "But of course, you are too." She patted Matt's arm.

"Sure I am," he agreed smiling, "but the only instrument I can play is a radio."

"Good enough," Dan agreed. "We have a meeting next month and I declare I don't know how we are going to handle five kids this time. Both sets of twins are all over the place."

"You mean, you will be leading in a revival, and Ellen playing piano?" Marigold thought a minute. "We could help. How far is it? We can keep them home or travel with you, can't we Matt?"

CHAPTER 5

RUTHIE

"You are happy." Ruthie watched Jewel cleaning the windows and the glass fronts of the cabinets, while she dust the furniture. "I bet you have a date with that Evan fellow." She saw Jewel grin. "I'm right."

"It's not a date, actually. If your mother doesn't care he is going to teach me how to play the guitar. I know a little but there's so much I don't know. The only thing, is, I don't know if I should go there."

"So you are grinning because of the music. Hmm." Ruthie continued dusting the furniture, ready to go into the next room. "Music makes me happy, too, but I don't grin all the time, I must be missing something. As far as going to Evan's house, if you feel uncomfortable about it, maybe you shouldn't."

"How old are you, to come up with all this wisdom and heavy duty teasing?"

"Does it offend you? I'll stop if it does. I share your joy but you are so quiet, I hope it's joy."

"Ruthie, you are so different." She finished the double windows and started on the door. "Will she care?

"I don't think so, unless she already made plans to go grocery shopping, then she'll ask you to have him come here because she will be leaving the twins with us."

"Oh, that would be even better, then you would be around if conversation lags. I like that better."

The phone rang and Ruthie answered. "Oh, Marigold. I can't. I'm pretty sure Momma's going to get groceries, it's the day she usually goes." Ruthie giggled. "I'll miss you, too, Tinkerbell."

Jewel's hand stopped mid-air, "Marigold's last name is Tinkerbell?"

"No, Silly. Her husband calls her that because used to Marigold wore leggings and tunics and bells that jingled. She was so much fun. Now she has two babies and she dresses different."

"Like me?" A serious note crept into Jewel's voice. "I don't know how to dress in these homemade skirt and blouses, Ruthie. I don't own a pair of jeans and I wish I did, but we never have the money for extras."

"Well, you will have spending money while you are here, maybe you could buy a few things you want."

"Oh, no, you are giving me a room until my parents find a place to live. I couldn't take any money."

"Momma and Daddy will work that one out with you Jewel. Where are your parents?"

"They are staying in the next town with a family that used to live out where we did."

"Did you want to stay with them, too?"

"I did, but they have five children and one more person meant one more bed and your parents had drawn my name so I came here."

As Ruthie suspected, it was grocery shopping day. Ellen ask Ruthie and Jewel to watch the boys while she was gone during lunch. Ruthie told her mother of Jewels invite to learn guitar, "but Momma, Jewel would be happy for Evan to come here if you don't care. She doesn't think it looks nice for her to be alone at Evan's home when she doesn't know him that well."

"The question is, can Evan last here in this house with two sets of twins who are constantly on the move?" Ellen hugged Ruthie as she turned to leave. "We'll finish your homework when I return. Just remember when the twins waken from their nap to keep an eye on them and the doors locked."

Jewel smiled. "I love your twins, Mrs. Gates; they aren't that hard to sit. I am pleased to watch them and Ruthie seems to do all the work."

"Then call Evan, if you wish and tell him the situation. It is up to him whether he comes or not and you are welcome to use the music room if you wish. I have a feeling you two are composers."

Ruthie clapped her hands. "Do you have a piano, Jewel?" She had no more ask than Ruthie apologized. "I'm sorry, Jewel, I forgot you lost everything in the flood."

"It's all right, Ruthie. I've never had anyone treat me as good as your family treats me. I will always remember this." She sighed. "I used the church piano to practice but I do in fact still have my keyboard."

"Are your parents very strict, Jewel?" Ruthie was seeing an older couple in her mind that loved their daughter but seldom laughed. "Do they laugh and did they play with you when you were little?"

"They love me, Ruthie, sometimes I think too much because it's hard for them to let go but my parents come from a Quaker background where little emotion is shown and too, they were older when they had me than most parents. I often wonder if they are so afraid they will lose me they can't loosen up. Does what I'm saying make any sense to you?"

"I know they love you and they love the Lord," Ruthie replied, "but Momma says sometimes we just have to trust the Lord and allow him to work things out." A memory came to mind, "I was kidnapped when I was little and my Momma says that was her biggest challenge ever and all she could do was trust God to take care of me wherever I was and when I was returned unharmed all she could do was thank Him and praise His name. I guess everyone has sad times and I listen to my Momma when she speaks to people and she always says when you don't understand, praise the Lord anyway because he is listening."

"Oh, Ruthie, you could have been killed or never seen your family again," There were tears in Jewels' eyes. "Your family loves the Lord like he's a member of the family, Ruthie. It's so real I feel your love for God. I really think God allowed me to spend time with your family and see his love in action because I need it so much. It's the joy that fills your heart that speaks to me and I love it."

Ruthie giggled. "I think you forgot to call Evan. He's coming up the walk to take you to learn guitar."

"Oh, Ruthie, let me go comb my hair and where do I put this dust cloth and where is the music room?"

"Hurry, I'll let him in and he does have his guitar, I believe, anyway he has a big case in his hand."

The winter days lengthened into spring with Easter Lilies making their first showing and in a weeks' time the tulips and Ruthie waited to hear the news from Newhaven where Pastor Levi and Leah waited for their first child. Marigold was the one to call Ruthie, "Guess what, my little apprentice?" Ruthie fell for it. "You are dancing in the recital this year." Marigold laughed. "No, something grand has happened in the little town of Newhaven." Ruthie jumped up and down. "Leah had her baby. The tulips are blooming, it's on time." They were happy for Leah and Levi. "Aren't you going to ask what it is?" Now, Ruthie laughed. "I've known all along. It's a boy. And right now they are trying to decide whether he is Jeremiah or Zedekiah. But he's so little they may call him Jimmy." Marigold was quiet a moment on the phone, "Are you kidding me?" Ruthie's laughter spread across the mile to Marigold in her shop. "Wait and see, they will name him Jeremiah Isaiah Merkal and call him Jim a few days then they'll start calling him Jeremiah." The silence was deafening, until finally Marigold said, "I got it, the initial of each name. Right? When do you want to go see the new baby boy, Little Jeremiah?" Giggling, Ruthie said, "Saturday, but I know you have plans, and I have to sit the twins next Sat. Let's go as soon as we can."

Jewel stood in the hallway listening to the phone conversation and wondering at Ruthie's happiness. She couldn't help but feel a sadness knowing soon, surely very soon, her parents would go to the house they had found on the outer edge of the Cape with enough acreage to plant a garden and she would be expected home. Her father decided it was time for him to retire, but whether to rent the farm to another farmer or sell it was still under consideration. Keeping the farm meant a yearly income, selling it would see them through retirement into the years of declining health if they planned wisely.

Without a vehicle, Jewel was helpless to find employment. She was unsure about her place in the family unit. The time of separation had driven home her desire to find another job, finish the last months of classes that had been put on hold and find an apartment of her own. How to tell her parents was the other thing. Staying with the Gates had shown her so many things were possible in life that she had felt foreign and impossible to attain. It was all a bit scary going into the world alone but she must.

Evan would be leaving soon. Word had it that the bridge to where Evan lived would be finished in another month. She could never say it but she would miss him. He was a good man; some of the sadness left his eyes when they played music together. She had learned more about the guitar but it was not her chosen instrument. The piano served that purpose. Once in admiring Evan's guitar, he had said, "thank you, I made it." Astonished, she questioned him further and found that was how he made his living. A number of Nashville stars had purchased from Evan.

"Have you thought of moving to Nashville?" She asked. He gave her a puzzled glance.

"Why would I do that?" For a moment indignation shined in his eyes. "I am not cut out for big city life."

That was the most unsettling moment she experienced with Evan. "I only meant to say there probably would be more people interested in your work, your guitars." He relaxed. "But if you build them I'm sure they will come to you," she teased, thinking of the line in Field of Dreams. Evan smiled. "I like your smile," she said. He slowly shook his head, and she could not read the expression on his face.

The time of their leaving seemed to be escalating. "I will miss seeing you, Evan and your wonderful music. Your music goes round in my head, especially the one you have written, Wishful Thinking."

"I wrote that for you."

"You did?" She was astonished. "Why didn't you tell me?"

"I thought you would know when you heard the words."

"Sing it for me." He appeared hesitant, then with the guitar began an opening and sang.

"When you wake up in the morning and see the bright blue sky, Do you ever think of me, do you ever wonder why…the good Lord up above us made the mountains oh, so high so we'd walk in hidden valleys when our hearts were sad to cry and we'd never know the reason….til we're old and then we die…Wishful thinking, wishful thinking, in the morning when the sun comes up I wonder where you are…and I climb the highest mountain and I touch the nearest star When you wake up in the morning do you ever think of me…. wishful thinking, wishful thinking, Oh, if it could ever be.. I would thank the Lord above us there you are… there you are…you are with me…wishful thinking, wishful thinking"

"Oh, Evan, that is wonderful, the most wonderful gift anyone has ever given me. Thank you." There were tears running down her cheeks. Evan reached up and wiped them away.

"Please, don't be sad."

"I'm not, I'm happy. It was just so touching that you would write that for me. I've never been very sure of myself. I guess I'm still not. But that was really nice, Evan."

"Will you marry me?" He spoke so softly, Jewel wasn't certain if she heard correctly. She was frozen.

"Did you ask me to marry you, Evan?"

"Yes." The gentlest of smiles began, but he was afraid of what she would say. "I did, will you marry me?"

"Yes, oh, yes, Evan." She threw her arms around him, hugging him and the guitar. "Do you mean it?"

"Yes. Or I would not have asked."

"When?"

"As soon as we can return to my home. But there may be mud in the house. I've not been able to get in."

"There's so much to think about, Evan and we have to tell my parents." Suddenly it hit her. "Evan. You have to ask my father for my hand in marriage. I thought no one would ask me, we've never discussed if someone did."

"Will your father be angry?"

* * * * * * *

"What? Daniel stared at Ellen. "Go over that again; I don't believe I heard you right."

"They are perfect for each other." Ellen couldn't understand his reaction. "Think about it."

"I am," Dan said glumly. "I think I better call them in here and do a quiz test." Ellen was grinning.

"Do it." Ellen went to the door of the music room. "Hey, you two, come into the kitchen, Dan has a few questions to throw at you." Her smile widened. "Don't be afraid, he's harmless but feels he must talk to you. Are you both all right with that? He's putting his long white beard on. Don't be scared."

"Actually, I was washing my hands." He started to sit at the opposite end of the table. "Now, I understand congratulations are in order. Congratulations." He leaned over and shook Evan's hand, then kissed Jewel on the cheek. "Is this love at first sight or what do we call it?"

Jewel spoke, "I think we grew into each other. Practicing daily, talking somewhat, well, I talked."

"Have you even kissed each other? Or said I love you?"

"No," they said together.

"I suggest you remedy that, not now, but before Evan returns home." Dan scratched his head. "I mean, what if you don't even like each other and the kiss is terrible?"

"We didn't know that a kiss was that important, did we?" She turned to Evan shaking his head. "No."

"Where will you live?"

"In his house," She said. He said, "In my house."

"Does anyone have a job?"

"He builds guitars. I plan to find a job, possibly in a store."

"What about your education?"

"I'll have to work awhile and save money before I start."

"I have some money," Evan interrupted, "When I build a guitar, someone in Nashville has signed up for it and the man who sells it out of his instrument store deposits it to my account." Evan was tugging at the wallet in his back pants pocket. "Here," He handed

Daniel a card. "Could you call and give them the account number and see if there's any money there?"

"Why don't you do it, Evan?"

"I don't know how, I've never had to before."

"I will but don't let anyone else. You can learn how to do this. Someone else might drain your account."

A ladies voice answered. "Who's calling, please?" Daniel placed the phone in front of Evan. "Evan Jacobs." "Your account number please?" With the card in front of his face, Jacob called off the numbers. "For security purposes what was your first grade teacher's name?" Evan smiled. "Missus Dorothy Gipson." Daniel was shocked. "That's correct sir, I'm pulling up your account, sir." They all waited patiently. "Sir, the amount is one hundred twenty thousand and thirty two cents. I'm glad you called, sir. You need to use your account occasionally or there will be a service charge on it." Daniel was leaning sideways his eyes large as saucers as he held the phone in front of Evan one last time. "Thank you, ma'am." Daniel and Ellen were smiling. "Thank you, sir, have a blessed day."

Daniel placed the phone in the cradle, raised his hand in a high five and Evan slapped it. "You are the man," Daniel exclaimed. "Did you really not know how much money you had in your account?"

"I figured a thousand or two but not that much."

"How many guitars have you built that the person is depositing money into your account?"

Evan thought a moment, "Well, There were seven last year and this year, three to singers and one small one for one of the men's son. I was just giving them away until this gentleman saw mine; he talked me into letting him sell them."

"Man, you are doing all right. I'm proud of you." Daniel caught Ellen's eye. She was beaming. "How many do you think you can make in a year?"

"Ten, maybe twelve, all depends on a good supply of the right kind of wood and the weather some what."

Daniel and Evan were discussing finances but Jewel asked a different question. "Was there one that stayed in your mind more than the other, for any reason?"

"Well, there's this lady dresses in pink, has pink hair and drives a pink car. She ordered one and It had to be pink. She left a piece she cut off the sleeve of her dress the color it had to be." He smiled remembering, "But she wanted rhinestones around the sound hole, I thought they were rhinestones she left, come to find out she had trusted me with fifty thousand dollars' worth of diamonds she wanted fit down into the wood."

"What's the next step?" Ellen asked. The two newly intended looked at each other. Evan replied, "I have to ask her father's permission to marry. How will that go, Jewel?"

"I don't know, I think my parents believe I'll be with them forever."

"You want to go this afternoon, I can drive you." Daniel turned to Ellen, "you don't need me, do you, Hon?"

"Your aunt is coming to take the twins and Ruthie to her house. If you wait until she picks them up, I'll ride with you, I've never had the pleasure of going with someone asking for his beloved's hand in marriage. It's exciting. Do you two mind?"

"We'd be honored," they replied, together.

* * * * * *

CHAPTER 6

The visit with Jewel's parents ended. Daniel drove home. Everyone was quiet as they dropped the two intended off at Anne and Andrew's. "We need to tell them," Evan said, "they've been nice to me."

"That was very interesting," Dan said, once they cleared the distance and he felt he could speak.

"It was enlightening." Ellen added.

"Did you get the part, Jewel's father was willing to put her through college if she remained with them, and cared for them in old age."

"Perhaps that is the Quaker way and they are getting older. It's called looking forward."

"No," Daniel disagreed, "It isn't the Quaker way at all. It's called not thinking and selfish. Jewel deserves a life of her own. Now I understand why she has little self-esteem and doesn't feel worthy of anything."

"She's learning. She turned the whole thing around very nicely, no backtalk at all. She managed to set a wedding date."

Daniel groaned, "At your expense. You just couldn't keep quiet, could you? Now you have refreshments to drum up and it looks like it will be a large crowd of people. It's not the cost, my love, what worries me is you, whether you are up to it, or not."

"It will be a delight."

"You are sounding more like Ellen Gates, that woman everyone talks about, the one who has two sets of twins, does book studies, fills in at the hospital when they need an RN and believes firmly in prayer. It is my opinion, that woman doesn't know how to settle down."

"She sounds like a real corker." They laughed together. "Oh, Daniel, won't a May wedding be beautiful in our garden?"

* * * * * *

By coincidence, Jewel was paid the next Friday and though she persisted in saying room and board was what was agreed on and that she would gladly help wherever she was placed, Ellen said she was good as gold watching the twins and must accept payment. On Saturday, Marigold and Ruthie took Jewel clothes shopping. "Nothing frivolous with bells on it for our Jewel," Ellen warned the two. "She is a no-nonsense person. Make her attractive, low key, don't flaunt her new found self, let her glow naturally."

They found she was a muted color candidate. Her first clothes were a white organza blouse with a proper camisole under, a peach colored pair of trousers with a matching crocheted vest. The second was an aqua colored dress with three quarter sleeves, a princess neckline and a bell skirt. Ruthie brought a simple pearl necklace for adornment. With Easter a Sunday away, Marigold found a periwinkle dress with matching jacket that had a bead encrusted ecru collar, adding a pair of crème colored shoes and a small purse. "You will be smashing, darling," she crooned, "but we must count our remaining loot."

The three beamed when it was decided there was enough left for two pair of blue jeans and three T-shirts." Finished, Marigold counted again. "We have spent two hundred thirty three dollars. You will have about seven dollars left," Marigold surmised, "But come work for me two evenings at the shop and you will begin building back. How does that sound?"

There were tears in Jewel's eyes. "I am overwhelmed. Thank you. I am so grateful." She hugged both.

It was Christmas all over when they returned to show Ellen their finds. "I must say, Marigold, I am impressed." Marigold danced a little jig and ended up putting a wet kiss on first, Ruthie's cheek, and then, Jewels.

"Gotta go," she said, smiling happily. "Matt's had enough baby time and I don't blame him."

* * * * * *

Anne's workweek had been demanding. Doctor Lonzo had been asked to take two patients that were refugees and could not speak English. She supposed due to that handicap the two showed up at the office each morning expecting Doctor Lonzo to examine them each day. It didn't make sense. She was the one left to deal with them; take their temperature, blood pressure, weigh them and try to explain the doctor was busy and could not see them. There was a genuine lack of understanding which meant all she could do was put them in a room from beginning to end of day, when they suddenly understood they must go home. Peering out the window to see Dr. Lonzo's car, if it was gone they went quietly. If, still there, their language flew through the office fluently, enough to make the remaining patients nervous.

"It makes no sense, Andrew," at end of day she felt quite irritable and tried not to pass it on to her family. "I'm almost to the point of believing there's a hidden motive we are blind to."

"What do they do in the rooms?"

"One room. They will not part from each other. They sleep."

"On the floor?"

"No, on the examining table. They are very thin and small. They wrap their arms around each other and sleep." Nothing made sense. They became quiet trying to think if there could be a hidden motive.

* * * * * *

"I need to call Marigold. Can you put the dishes in the dishwasher? I won't be long." She had fed the children before Andrew came home and thankfully they were asleep in their own beds. Dialing the house phone, she listened for Marigold.

"Hey, I saw your name. How are you?" Marigold's sounding cheerful only added to her unsettled spirit.

"What do you think about Evan and Jewel's plan to marry?"

"They seem quite happy. I was afraid they would be financially insecure but Dan said not to worry, they would be all right."

"I wouldn't ask and Andrew said it was none of our business, does he have a job, or at least a trade?"

"Dan says he builds guitars and they are beautiful. I don't know if that's enough but Dan said don't worry."

"Have they set a date? Our children were in full swing when they were here and we were not at our best."

"I heard May mentioned and that came from Ruthie."

"That's only a month away, Marigold. Will Evan be back in his own home by then?"

Marigold laughed. "Evan lives with you, Anne. Ask him. I meant in Andrew's office." She was quiet for a moment. "What's wrong, Anne? I hear it in your voice. You are always so calm."

"Problem at work," Anne confessed. "Dr. Lonzo and I are working on it."

"Can I help?"

"No. But thanks." She sighed. "Life is full, isn't it? I don't guess Matt's decided if he's farming this year?"

"I hope not, I can't take another year with these kids and him gone, since his mother tries to tie him and Britany together. He says no, but his dad still isn't well."

"Has Britany had her baby?"

"I would be the last to know…but I'm sure she will call Matt."

"Sorry I ask, remember I love you my friend, she may be my husband's partner's wife but Pookie is keeping awfully quiet, so we don't know if something's going on or not."

"Just so she stays away from my husband," Marigold replied. "Anne, try not to worry over Evan and Jewel. I think they have led such sheltered lives they will strive to make it together. They don't seem to have had material blessings and their hearts are pure. Jewel cries when someone does something nice for her and the sadness we all saw in Evan disappears when he's with her."

Taking a deep breath, Anne considered Marigold's advice. "All right, Marigold, I'll try."

"Come here, Anne," as she placed the phone on the cradle she heard Andrew call from the bathroom.

"What are you doing?" The room was saturated in steam. "Turn on the fan." Andrew was sitting on the bench to her dressing table. The tub was three fourths full of sudsy water and her bath salts container was in the corner of the tub.

"For you, sweet Anne, there's something bothering you besides the two patients you watch sleep all day and Evan and Jewel getting married." He sat there, a kind expression on his face and she couldn't help but think, this handsome man that had been drawn to another life in their first years of marriage had changed. "Come on, you need to soak and relax. I'm going to study a case momentarily and then maybe you will tell me what it is." Rising off the bench, he kissed her lightly on the lips and left the room. "I'll be in our room, if it's all right with you I'm going to stretch out on the bed. I'll read a bit as I wait for you."

She undressed and sank into the water. He had thought of everything. The neck pillow was on one end of the tub, her robe on the hook by the door. Was there any reason to worry him? She'd seen the woman again that questioned her at the Seminar; she had a strange feeling that woman was checking her out. It would not leave her mind the possibility there was a connection to Addy's mother…or possibly just Addy.

She soaked until her toes felt shriveled and glanced at the clock. Ten til nine. Andrew would be asleep. By the time she'd used lotion the tub had drained. She hung up the towel and turned off the light. He was sprawled across the bed, still wearing his white shirt and suit pants, a pencil in his hand where he'd written a few words on the note pad. She leaned down to read, *talk to the judge about this*. He was such a deep sleeper, she removed his socks, pulled his trousers off but decided there was no way she could remove his shirt. Flipping the switch on her side of the bed, the lights dimmed, she went in to check the children and came back to coax him onto his pillow and climbed into bed beside him. Even in sleep his arm went around her as he pulled her to his side. *I love you*, came muffled and soft. "I love you, too."

She had to put worry behind her. Life was full of coincidence. Their life was good. Finally, Andrew loved her and his children. Sweet Andy, precious Addy felt as much like her own as if she gave birth. *Thank you dear Lord, she whispered, and thank you for Andrew changing. God bless Dorothy and Harper for taking him in and showing him your way; if they hadn't and if Ellen hadn't been a shining example we probably wouldn't be together. There are so many people I appreciate, heavenly Father. Help us to grow in your love and to be an example to others as these have been to us. I love you, Lord. Bless our friends and those in need; bless Dr. Lonzo and Little Momma and his two little patients. Thank you. Amen.*

* * * * * *

EVAN

The following Sunday, Evan was up early, polishing his shoes, pressing his trousers, with an iron spraying a little starch in the sleeves of his shirt and rather stricken viewing the only sport coat he was able to salvage. His wardrobe was very limited. In truth, what he owned was water logged and he feared in bad need of replacement. He could hardly wait to see Jewel. He was taken by her the first time he laid eyes on her but he was shy and until she knew a person, so was she. He loved the tinkling sound of her laughter and the way her eyes came alive with tiny little crinkles at the corners. What, he wondered could she possibly see in him? Her parents hadn't seen anything worth wanting their daughter to marry him but she pressed right on through setting a wedding date while they scowled at her plans.

He had never kissed her, in fact his experience was limited to grade school years when Millie Duncan demanded he kiss her or she would tell the teacher she saw him peeing in the school's coat room. He should have let her tell because he hadn't and who would believe such a story. But he was a little boy, scared and kissed her. She then told him he was a terrible kisser and she hoped she didn't die from it, but he probably would. She seemed to be an authority on things he had never heard of. As he thought about it now, it was a wonder he was allowed to attend school. The piece of land, now flooded, that he lived on had been in the family since eighteen ninety seven according to his father, having belonged to the grandfather that fought in the civil war. They paid their taxes and didn't bother anyone. It was a sort of refuge he supposed, based on his own father coming there. He supposed it would be all right for him to marry. All the relatives had died. There was no one to stop him. For all the secrecy of the family, they loved music and most could play about any instrument they chose.

He rode to church sitting in the third seat of Andrew's new suburban. He knew he should say something. "This is nice, Andrew."

"We were getting cramped in Anne's little blue Chevrolet and I was exhausted driving Harriet's antique. The thing reminded me of a tank and I will admit it saved my life once when Walden's men came after me." He laughed. "Of course you weren't here to know, it was like having the mob after you. We had reached a point we had to consider safety factors with two car seats for the children. Andy's almost ready for a booster seat. What do you drive, Evan?"

"All I have is an old forty eight Ford truck. It runs like a top but getting it stuck when the water was coming in and no one to pull it out wasn't the wisest thing I could have done."

"Are you thinking of looking for another vehicle?"

"We have to." Evan smiled thinking of Jewel. "With a wife I want to take care of her."

"That's nice, Evan," Anne glanced back to see his smile. "Really nice," she repeated.

They filed in to Christ Church and found a seat behind the group. They were growing, sometimes it took two pews. The song service began and flowed, touching hearts with joyful singing. It was when Pastor Joe said, "Turn around and wish your brother or sister in Christ a good day. Let's make everyone feel welcome to Christ Church." Anne turned with her hand out to come face to face with the lady from the seminar who had ask the question and then left.

Anne's smile froze on her face. "We are happy to have you worship with us," she began but the expression on the woman's face did not appear as the usual person coming to worship. Anne wasn't sure what her mission was but she turned back to her seat, wondering if the family should move.

Now she faced the row in front of her family. Dorothy and Harper Gipson turned to hug her and shake Andrew's hand. Dorothy gave her a once over, then asked, "What is wrong? I can tell by your expression. Have you had bad news?" Harriet sit next to Dorothy, Now she was studying Anne. "What's going on?" A hand on Anne's arm, Harriet whispered, "We'll get to the bottom of it after church." All Anne could do was nod. She was experiencing an icy fear that was turning her body into an ice cold paralysis. As if he felt her anxiety, Andrew reached for her hand and held it until services ended.

"Friends, Let us continue to stand for the reading of today's scripture. Turn to Matthew chapter twenty six; verses thirty six through forty five. ON this Sunday before Easter let us," Pastor Joe was saying. "begin the story that means everything to our belief in the Lord." *Then cometh Jesus with them unto a place called Gethsemane and saith unto the disciples, Sit ye here, while I go and pray yonder. And he took with him Peter and the two sons of Zebedee and began to be sorrowful and very heavy. Then saith he unto them, "My soul is exceedingly sorrowful, even unto death; tarry ye here and watch with me." And he went a little farther and fell on his face and prayed saying, O, my Father, if it be possible, let this cup pass from me, Nevertheless not as I will but as thou wilt." And he cometh unto his disciples and findeth them asleep and saith unto Peter. What could ye not watch with me one hour? Watch and pray that ye enter not into temptation; the spirit indeed is willing but the flesh is weak. He went away the second time, and prayed, saying, O my Father, if this cup may not pass away from me, except I drink it, thy will be done. And he came and found them asleep again; for their eyes were heavy. And he left them, and went away again, and prayed the third time, saying the same words. Then cometh he to his disciples and saith unto them, sleep on now and take your rest; behold the hour is at hand and the Son of Man is betrayed into the hands of sinners. Rise, let us be going; behold he is at hand that doth betray me."*

"Never," Brother Joe began, "Was Jesus more human than during the time he faced death. He felt the sadness of betrayal. He trembled with knowledge the men could kill him at any moment." Pastor Joe leaned across the podium, his eyes on the center aisle. "Let me step away from the scene from the Bible for a moment. Some of you have faced and many of you will a moment in your life when you realize you are in the company of a person who's intent is to do you harm, whether bodily harm or killing your spirit. Who will you rely on? Do you know the Lord? That is the most important question you will face today. Jesus knew he was facing death, when you read the words from the Bible you will understand, just because he was the Son of God he was not exempt from pain and sorrow. Wasn't he grieving enough knowing his disciples would betray him? Would you grieve the Savior of your soul? Do we understand his worries? He had walked daily with these men, allowed them to see who he was. Now he is worried whether the disciples are strong enough to face the world. You notice he ask the disciples to keep watch. Three times he asked they keep watch as he prayed. Three times he prayed the same prayer. When you pray down on your knees, is one thing but if as Jesus did, you fall on your face praying, does that mean you are in desperate need of an answer? Jesus heart was in the action. But what happens after he prays the second time? "O my Father, if this cup may not pass away from me, except I drink it, thy will be done." He has accepted what is at hand. He knows he will be scorned, whipped, spit upon, not for himself but for us. Betrayal is at hand. When life hands you or me a discouraging task, do you think we can say not my will, but thy will be done? What does it take to reach acceptance?" Brother Joe stepped down from the pulpit. "If you or I have not experienced the bitter dregs of disappointment we can rest assured that it will touch our lives sooner or later. We do not have the heart of our Savior but our heart needs the Savior. Christ died for us, no greater love than He lay down his life for our sins. But you and I have to make the decision whether we will follow him. One thing is certain, when death comes whether expected or suddenly with no warning, we will have settled the question, where will I spend eternity. There will be no turning back. At that moment where we spend eternity no longer lingers for discussion. It is finished. Turn in your hymnals to page three hundred seventy; Never Alone. Pastor Joe gave ample time for the altar call, and then it was time to dismiss. "Next Sunday we will discuss the cross," he said. "Now let us close with prayer."

"I've seen the lightning flashing and heard the thunder roll; I've felt sin's breakers dashing, trying to conquer my soul…" The singing was sounding as though each person was considering not only the words of the song but the scripture…"The world's fierce winds are blowing, temptations are sharp and keen…"

Even the children were quiet on the ride home. Evan had asked if Jewel could ride with them. "We are a half a dozen," Andrew remarked as the two climbed into the back seats and he and Anne settled Addy and Andy into their seats. "Do you two have anything in mind for lunch?"

"From your house we are walking to Miss Harriet's," Evan replied. "She said she has something she wants us to see and she asked if we would have a light lunch with her."

Andrew had quite a laugh. "I can almost imagine what Harriet has in mind, but I won't ruin the surprise. How about we drive by, the air is a little nippy today."

"Jewel, you look lovely in your blue dress. Ellen told me Marigold went shopping with you." She heard Jewel say thank you and glanced around to see Evan smiling at her. "You look nice too, Evan."

Watching the two walking up Harriet's drive, Anne couldn't help but ask, "What do you think it is?"

His laughter had a ring of happiness in it. "I declare, she is bent on ridding herself of that big old tank we all call a car. If I were a betting man, I'd put my money on her asking Evan if he would like to use it, or she may even give it to him. One thing for certain, they don't make cars that hold up like that one anymore."

For the first time, Anne smiled. Andrew leaned over to kiss her. "That's my girl. Do you have something to tell me?"

"Yes, I do." They carried the children in, lay them on their beds, removed their shoes and lay a light blanket over them. "Thank you for not insisting we eat with the group today. I wasn't up to it. So now let's go in the kitchen and have a sandwich and I'll tell you."

"Let me get this straight," Andrew said, peering up from spreading mayonnaise on two slices of bread. "The women sitting behind you ask the question at the Seminar and today she was unfriendly and you feel she is tracking you. Why?"

"It's a feeling that she means us some kind of ill intent. Not everyone knows you are Addy's biological father, I'm not sure that's it, but she is pursuing our having her, I realize I've seen her watching us other times."

"Where?"

"The grocery store, the bank, and just strolling down the street in our own neighborhood."

"Sweetheart, have you ever heard the expression, let sleeping dogs lie?" He glanced at Anne.

She replied, "Yes, but this one is not asleep."

* * * * * *

A few days later a Police car pulled up in front of the house. The officer came up the walk and knocked on the door. Anne hesitated but he saw the bell's button and pushed it. Anne opened the door.

"Mrs. Anne Graves?" He handed her a package. "You have been served."

Immediately she called Andrew. "What does this mean, Andrew?" She was distraught. "Yes, just now and he said, Mrs. Graves you have been served."

"We will have to get a lawyer and go to court, Anne. It's bound to be about Adeline. Someone wants custody of her."

"You are a lawyer, Andrew." Now she was crying. "We might lose Addy, Andrew." That caused Andrew's anger to surface.

"I'm her father, Anne. Summer gave her to you. Don't you think if she had any feelings for her mother she would have given Addy to her?" Anne's sobs increased.

"You think it's Summer's mother? She's rich. She can buy and sell us ten times over. We have nothing to go against her, Andrew."

He grew quiet letting her settle down. "Anne, for the first time in our lives we do have something. We have each other, and two precious children and we intend to keep them. God is with us, Anne, don't let go, let's help each other to keep the faith."

"It's hard, Andrew, I'm so scared. I love Addy."

"I know Sweetheart, and I love you even more for taking her. I treated you so bad, Anne. What would I do if you hadn't forgiven me?" He grew quiet remembering. "I'll be home soon."

CHAPTER 7

HALEY

Ruthie was sitting the table when the phone rang. Ellen hurriedly wiped the flour off her hands and answered. "Gates Residence."

"Ellen, it's me, Haley. Are you busy, tomorrow?"

"Just the usual day, as far as I know. Can I help you with something?"

"If you have someone to sit the twins, I would like for you and Marigold to meet me on the Southside of town at that new Restaurant Millees at noon. Is that possible?"

"Ruthie," She had finished sitting the table and left the room. "Ruthie." Ellen could hear her playing with the twins. "Just a minute, Haley, I have to walk down the hall to see if I have a sitter. I'm laying the phone down." She found Ruthie with Jewel. Jewel was teaching the older twins how to write their name on small standing blackboards. "Girls, are you free to sit the twins tomorrow from eleven til two?" Both nodded and Ellen smiled, "I'll work with you on your homework before I go, Ruthie."

Returning to the phone, she said, "Yes, Haley, that will be nice. Do you want me to call Marigold or can you?" Ellen laughed. "Yes, with Jewel here, the house is quieter. I home school Ruthie and when Jewel works with the twins they feel so important. They call it their homeschool. But Jewel's time with us is ending soon and we will sorely miss her. Yes, we can catch up tomorrow. See you then."

Within the hour Marigold called. "Hey, Ellen, you want to ride with me tomorrow to meet Haley? Yes, I can still call Caroline to watch the shop. Harriet's got her hands full with four kid-do's."

* * * * * *

The twins were in bed. Ruthie and Jewel were finishing cleaning the bathroom where the boys had a splashing party. "I'm telling you, those two works together so well and are such a help to me, I will miss Jewel when she leaves." She turned to Daniel. "You are really quiet tonight. Is something wrong at work?"

"No, not at work but something is wrong for our friends and it concerns me greatly."

"I haven't heard." She thought of Haley's problem. "Who is it?"

"Anne was served papers yesterday on Addy to start a custody suit. Andrew called today to talk about it. He's a lawyer and he's worried. Evidently it is Summer's mother although they were estranged."

"Oh, no, Anne must be devastated. You would think she gave birth to that child."

"Andrew said they have to counter file or the Judge would think they were uninterested and default against them. They are getting their information together. There has to be a financial disclosure."

"Summer's mother won't mind that, she is probably the richest woman in the Cape, next to Harriet."

"Harriet can't help them here, although I know she would but the numbers have to be already in effect."

"If they counter the filing will their papers have to be served to Mrs. Walden?"

"Yes, that's the way it works and hope that the judge hasn't ordered anything yet. Play fair, so to speak."

"There's something else," Ellen stretched out on her side of the bed. "Haley asked Marigold and me to meet her for lunch tomorrow and it concerns me what this is going to be about. I know by now her bruises will have healed and hopefully she has been able to accept what happened, but I've read women never accept being raped and who can expect them too? Anyway, I don't know if she made Jeremy believe she was with Marigold or not. It's a tangled mess. I kind of dread it."

Daniel reached for her hand. "Let's pray about this."

"Heavenly Father, our hearts are burdened for our friends but Lord we thank you for a good day in our lives that our family is intact, no one is ill and we come to you asking forgiveness for any wrong we've done. Help us Lord, to be mindful of others concerns, to care and keep them lifted to your grace and mercy. Be with our children, Lord and with us that our minds are clear and we trust in you. Amen.

MILLIEES RESTAURANT

"Wow." Marigold glanced around. "This place is upscale to most in the Cape. Wonder who owns it?"

"Kind of looks like it stepped out of the movies, what was the name of that one that had the black and white tiles, the mirrors on the walls…her name was Daisy…it was one of the classics…oh, I don't know."

"There was a yellow car, what did they call them in those days? Roadster? Oh, there she is, in the corner." Marigold leaned to kiss Haley on the cheek, then stood back to study her. "You look good."

Ellen gave her a hug and they all shared a smile, whether of relief or the fact things were better than they ever hoped. "Cool place," Ellen said. "I never knew it was here."

"So why are we here?" Marigold was always one to get to the reason. "How are you besides looking good?"

Haley held up her hand. "Let's order before we get into the reason." She saw Marigold's eyebrows raise at the menu prices. "I'm buying lunch. I made a sale and it's a good one." She glanced around the room. "They usually don't seat anyone close unless the place is crowded." She took a deep breath. "Okay, it has been painful and has had an effect on my marriage, not to mention I thought I was going to have a nervous breakdown, but I also had to face facts. If Jeremy found out, I would probably lose my marriage and I had better have a job or at least funds to fall back on. I have made myself go forward and it has not been easy. I have literally dragged myself out of bed mornings to go to work and I look over my shoulder to see who's following me. I think I had to ask you to meet me, most of all for support."

"Have you regretted not telling Jeremy you were raped?" Ellen shuddered at the word. "I'm sorry."

"Never." Sadness crept into Haley's expression as she stared down at her lap. When she raised her eyes, they were pools of darkness. "I couldn't tell you that night…it was…" She seemed unable to finish the sentence. "It was Jeremy's father and it wouldn't matter who it was, I'm afraid Jeremy would kill him."

"In all truth, I think we both wondered if it was him. But you are certain Jeremy knows nothing?"

"Too much was going on that night. I later found out his dad left the house in a drunken rage; Jeremy and his mother were out hunting him. He left a trail, bar to bar but they lost him when he got to the Cape. They were scared to death he would get hurt."

"Jeremy was in the Cape?" Marigold felt the worry of Jeremy knowing but not saying he did. "So how did his Father arrive here? Did he drive? Because they could track his car, couldn't they?"

"I nearly worried myself sick over that, Marigold. But Kathryn was desperate to find him. I was in a company car that night and there were at least five others parked around the motel. I didn't go home because I was to show another property the next morning." Her words ebbed away as she finished. "Until I got the heel of my shoe hung and fell and hit those boulders." She shook her head. "I feel so sad that I have to do this…but Jeremy would cut his dad out of his life."

Ellen thought of the stories Anne had told her of growing up and some of the drunken brawls the family had; she had to rely on her stepfather and to the present never really knew her mother or where she lived. "How are things with Jeremy and his dad?"

"It's difficult, Kathryn and Jonathan are separated. Where do you go on weekends to see your parents when everything's up in the air? He is as unsettled as I am and I have much more reason and we can't even talk about it."

"What else, Haley?" Haley's eyes never left Marigold as she sat there; the words spinning around and around in her head. "What is it you cannot share with Jeremy?"

Haley reached for their hands, thankful the table was small and there they sit, their hands making a circle. "I've missed my period." Her eyes filled with tears. "I dreamed of having Jeremy's baby and then this happened and now ..." A sob caught in her throat. "I'm already living a lie. I haven't told my husband and if I did I don't' think he could handle it; if I want any life at all with Jeremy I cannot tell him."

"Haley," Ellen searched for the right words, "Haley, there are circumstance that make women miss their period and stress is one and you have certainly had enough stress. Many times a month isn't enough. You have to give it more time. A doctor would tell you that. Did you go and did he tell you that?"

"Yes," she said as they tightened the grip of their hands and their heads dropped to study the tabletop.

Ellen glanced around; the room was empty of people. "Let us pray. Father, Heavenly Father, we are yours, you are ours, help us to understand what has happened and the consequence that falls on Haley though she is innocent of blame and her desire is to keep a family together. Neither Jeremy nor Kathryn would see beyond their own hurt at this time. You are Lord of all, only you can make things right. Now we ask you to strengthen Haley in this great task she has undertaken, be with Jeremy to see beyond the confusement of his parent's separation and Lord bring reason to his parents to fight for their marriage as Haley is willing to fight for hers. We thank you for friendship to share and ask you to help us be there for each other. We love you and praise you and look to you for guidance. Now, Lord forgive us where we fail you. In your gracious name. Amen.

They were walking to their vehicles when Marigold stopped. "Ellen, if Haley should be pregnant and a DNA test was run on the baby and someway using DNA from both father and son; would their DNA be the same?" Haley was listening intently, her hand on Ellen so firm, the three stopped walking.

"Are you asking if Jeremy and his father's DNA would be the same? You have to take into consideration Jeremy will also have DNA from his mother, but that being said, there could be a false reading that some lab technicians would let pass by and a family would never question it."

"I wish. I hope. I pray," Haley murmured. "I thought having to go to prison when I was not guilty was the worst thing would ever happen to me but the worry this has caused is worse."

Marigold and Ellen hugged Haley and told her to stay in touch. "I love you girls," she said. "Thank you."

"This is one of life's situations you wonder why it had to happen," Ellen mused out loud. "Throughout the Bible, stories of heart break remind us over and over since Adam and Eve sinned in the garden, such will always be with us."

"Things got worse after they sinned, didn't it? Cain killed Able." Marigold was troubled over Haley's problem. "Does Haley really think Jeremy would kill a man for raping her?"

"What would be Matt's first instinct?" Ellen shrugged. "I don't know, Marigold, but men usually say they would and yet as Christians we are to forgive."

"It's hard to decide which man responds, the Christian man or the natural father in a man when they hear of such and if it is a child, they hardly slow down their anger burns so hot but doesn't ours, as mothers? Are we thinking Haley is doing all she can and in the process it is a lifetime secret and we have to keep it, too?"

"Yes, we are. It is not a problem for me, is it you?"

"No, if it were me I might have to do the same, but who knows how a man reasons things out. I'll tell you why I said that. This thing of Matt returning to help his father get the crop out, leaving us is a hardship and if he goes this year it will be the third time." Marigold eased out onto the main street, by-passing a funeral procession lined up in a church yard. "If he would stand up to his mother," she continued, "when she says, would you leave us without help when your father is unable to work? Matt would tell his parents, you can rent the land out a couple years until Dad is better or you might decide you like the freedom, but what Vivien is doing is infringing on her son's home life because he is there more than with his children and me."

"Are you bitter, Marigold?"

"No, I can't afford to harbor those feelings; it would poison me but never affect the others. When I was sick and Matt wasn't there I delved in pity and found it isn't my nature. If I have to be alone, then I will do my best and try not to call on anyone else but it did put a division between us for a time."

"You are a strong woman, Marigold. Do you see any of Harriet in you?"

Marigold laughed. "Yes, my biological mother and I are stubborn as all get out. My adopted mother wasn't."

"All of us, in the group, wondered if you two would make it to a happy twosome as Mother and daughter."

"We butt heads but for the most part we've made it. Harriet is a grand old girl."

"Yes, she is. Do you love her like she is your mother?"

"Oh, yes." Marigold giggled. "Matt loves her too, when he calls her Ma, she likes it for all the pretending she doesn't. Yeah, if my adoptive parents had to die, I thank God for bringing Harriet into my life."

ATTORNEY ANDREW GRAVES

"I have to see Judge Springer," Andrew announced as Pookie was studying the address book for a certain Hutson Camp who owed the firm three thousand dollars.

"Here it is on Donaldson street. I'll get the statement mailed out to him, today. Go on, see the Judge."

"All right, see you later."

Andrew had called and was shown in immediately. "What brings you in, Andrew?" Judge Springer stood to shake hands and immediately sit back down.

"Judge, there's a custody case brewing over my little daughter, Addy. When Summer and I were together, she couldn't stand her mother or vice versa, she refused to live at home because her mother's husband was sexually abusing her and her mother either didn't care or didn't believe her. She lived her social life to the hilt. Mrs. Walden did, not Summer. Before Summer died, she brought Addy to my wife and gave her to us. I know she'd thought long and hard on it because she loved Addy so much. "

"I hate to tell you this, Andrew, but Mrs. Walden has requested custody of the child, already. It was a matter of telling you but you came in and made it easy."

"Why are you doing this, sir? I'm supposed to have fourteen days from the day the papers are served to get things in order. Those papers were served last Friday evening."

"Did you look at the date on the papers?" Without a blink of the eye the Judge predated the papers.

"Would you really take a child from parents that love her just to appease a rich woman?" Andrew saw the fire in the Judge's eyes. "Wasn't she your best supporter in years past? Do you feel you owe her?"

The Judge stood, "I cannot impress upon you the folly of your thinking. You should choose your words carefully. Your next case may appear before me, so tread carefully. You will have your day in court and you will have another thought, perhaps with no migraines."

"If I cannot appeal to you, my colleague, then who can I? We are desperate. This will break Anne's heart."

"You should have thought of that before you played around." The judge read what Mrs. Walden ask for concerning Addy. "You will have to pay child support to Mrs. Walden."

"She's the richest woman in town, Judge, are you kidding me?"

"It's the law, Andrew."

"The law seems to be what fits your discretion of the moment." Andrew gathered his papers and left.

The Judge picked up the phone and made the call to Family Services. "Did you receive my letter? I'll give you a call when its heads up. I'm thinking let them have the weekend and then Monday."

* * * * * * *

Andrew didn't go back to the office. He couldn't concentrate. He went home. The house was quiet without Anne and the children. He slipped out of his shoes and padded into Andy's room first and then Addy's. Sweet Adeline, he hummed. Little Addy was blonde enough to resemble Anne. Anne filled his mind now. Was he paying for all the times he treated her badly? She had always loved him, been kind to him. Where did she get the self-control? She said she didn't have it until she knew Ellen and was saved.

Anne would die without the children but no one was taking Andy. He took Andy from Anne. It was his fault Anne was crushed by the car and laid unconscious in the hospital for months. Bitty and Harriet were there every day. They took care of her. Harriet took her into her home as one would a daughter. She was there with Anne as she learned to walk again, bathe and dress herself. Dear Harriet loaned him that beast of a car but it saved his life. Harriet with the money she kept offering but they wouldn't take and now he had child support to pay to a woman who could buy the town. She didn't need his money and she wouldn't want Addy when Addy cried. Summer said her mother had no time for wasting a day. What could he do except tell Anne the truth. He knew the routine. The Judge would let them keep Addy over the weekend, then when he left for work, a social worker and the Family Service people would swoop in and take Addy, saying "it's all for the best, Mrs. Graves. Now kiss her goodbye. We have to go." Andrew sat on the end of Andy's bed and cried. What kind of mess had he made of their lives?

When the phone rang, he stumbled around, getting his bearings and reached it before it quit. "Andrew," Harper's voice rang through the empty house. "How you doin', Boyo?" Harper laughed his joyful laugh. "Me and Dorothy are missin' you all. What're you up to? You know we went down to see Haley and Jeremy, then this last week Dorothy had a class reunion and we missed church to go to that." Harper slacked off talking, he'd felt the silence. "What's wrong, Boyo?" He realized Andrew couldn't talk. "You cryin', Son?" His own voice took on a husky tone. "Just tell me what it is, so we can pray it through."

Andrew told him. Harper was quiet, listening to the end. "It all goes back to my treatment of Anne, Harper. Now we may lose Addy. Judge Springer is in Mrs. Walden's pocket. She made a big contribution and he's going to cater to her wants, wait and see. He said as much, but it would be my word against his and you know what that means." Andrew tried to clear his throat. "I'm the good for nothing boy grown to be a man that got religion and now they're waiting to see me give that up."

"His words were, *Mrs. Walden has already asked custody of her. You just made it easy coming in to see me. And I ask him would you take a little child from parents that love her and he replied, you should have thought about that before you played around and you will have to pay child support.*"

"That rascal," Harper's voice boomed. "We've known all along he catered to the rich and the poor be damned. That needs some lookin' into. I built homes for all those rich folks and some aren't like him. Let me do some investigatin.'"

"Harper if they take Addy all the investigating in the world won't help."

"Then we got to get on this first thing in the morning. What's the name of that judge me and you had? He straightened you out. We need to give him a lot of credit. Find his number."

So involved in conversation, Andrew didn't realize Anne had come in. She laid Andy in the big chair in the living room and tiptoed out for Addy asleep in her car seat. Then, she stood and listened. *Mrs. Walden has asked custody of her.* She knew when Andrew got off the phone. She knew he would take a long hot shower. Her mind was clear, her body went into motion. With both children lying asleep in the living room, she formed a plan. The children's medicines, extra shoes, clothes for a different climate, games, baby doll, her own clothes. Put the suitcases in the trunk of the car. Snacks in a different container. Birth certificates. Sunglasses. Swimming suits and sand shoes. Money.

She carried Andy first and then Addy, laid them in their bed, shoes off, blanket over, turned the light low in their bedrooms, and left a note on the kitchen counter top, *I had to run an errand real quick. I'm locking doors, kids are asleep. I love you and I'll be back soon.* She drove according to the speed limit knowing that would be a requirement, not just a law.

The lights were low when she turned into Dr. Lonzo's drive. She hurried to the door and rang the doorbell. Olivia, wearing a long robe, answered. "Anne." The door opened as did Olivia's arms. When Anne was properly hugged she pulled her into the room. "Poppa, look who has come to see us." Another hug and then the two stepped back to study their late night guest. "What's wrong?" They said in unison.

"Sit down and listen so you will understand. This is the most important thing you will hear from me." Tears brightened her eyes and she wiped them away. "Tonight I overheard Andrew talking to Harper Gipson, he's the one got down on the dirty bathroom floor with Andrew when Andy nearly died from the hit and run accident. Andrew was crying and this is what he said, "Judge Springer said Mrs. Walden wants custody of Addy and that Andrew will have to pay her child support. There was more, but the thing is she is rich, we are not and Judge Springer always accepted large contributions from her in his previous campaigns before he became a judge. He will do what she wants." Now Anne began to cry. "Addy's mother gave her to me because she had been watching me a long time she said and knew I was a good mother and a good person. And Andrew is the father and you know Addy looks just like Andy's baby pictures." Olivia was crying with Anne and handing over tissues.

Dr. Lonzo was thinking through what Anne had said. "What do you need?" His tongue was thick with the old world language. "Say and you will have it. You need money? Okay. You need different car, no one knows whose it is, you need a different name?"

Anne threw her arms around him. "Help me figure this out. I have to leave and I must not tell Andrew where I'm going and you haven't seen me. You have always said you love me and you know I wouldn't ask if I didn't love you the same but I never wanted to take advantage of your kindness or love for me and I would never until tonight I don't know what to do but if they take Addy I'll die."

"Do you want me to go with you?" Olivia's eyes were red from crying. "I could go, right, Poppa?"

"If you are gone and know nothing about Andrew's conversation with the Judge, what can they do? They will search for you." His words were powered by the energy circulating in his veins that this country could have such evil. Were it ever so in his own land, he asked himself and sadly shook his head, yes, yes. If this is done, it must be done right. Momma, where does that friend of yours live that offers you her home? On NCIS they put out an all-points-bulletin, I don't know what they do in the Cape."

Olivia's eyes were piercing as she looked across the room which had become a far away place where her friend lived. "You want I should go with you and help with the children?" Dr. Lonzo was smiling. "When I go to the medical convention, I will join you."

"Dr. Lonzo, we cannot talk on the phone."

"Anne. Anne." His hands were on her shoulders. "Trust me. We will find a way. Doctors hear things no one else wants to hear. There are phones that can be bought for cash with no contract. You use them awhile, replace them often to avoid leaving a trail and getting caught with them and if we use them wisely, short conversations and such, we avoid someone picking up our personal data." He kissed her forehead, "But we must not use a land line or our other phones. We will all have one and our conversations will be short and to the point." His eyes were kind watchful of this one he loved. "You understand, my Anne?"

"No surgery tomorrow, Poppa?" Olivia was asking.

"No, Momma. Tomorrow, Momma, you start to live a life of adventure. NSIC, I believe."

"No, Poppa, NCIS. Tomorrow, Anne, you will be beautiful in a different color hair. Yes?" She chuckled, "And I shall have short red hair. Yes, Poppa? No one will know us. I am Little Momma the grandmother and you, dear Anne are Momma with brown hair? Yes?" When Anne did not reply, but seemed not to understand, "You still have brown page boy wig from church program you showed me, Andrew wore being a disciple?"

"Oh, yes, Olivia, I do. Thank you. I didn't know what you meant." She hugged Olivia. "I must go." She hugged Dr. Lonzo. "I'm so sorry I won't be there to assist you in the next weeks. Please forgive me."

"You go with my blessing." There were tears in his eyes. "Soon, you understand how much we love you."

"You are willing to send Olivia with us, I know already." She hugged and kissed him on the cheek. "I'll make it up to you."

"Momma will be ready at the crack of dawn, if that is your wish. All else will be as discussed."

"Remember, you can't tell Andrew. As long as he doesn't know he can't tell. It's for his own safety."

"It is for his safety," Dr. Lonzo repeated. "Momma, we have work to do. Preparation."

* * * * * *

Driving home gave her time to think. She must make no mistakes. Taking Olivia would be a help with the children while at the same time incriminating her. Still, Dr. Lonzo encouraged his wife in going. Maybe together they would not have as many fears of losing Addy. Anne's heart ached, to leave Andrew when he was upset, to leave him alone to face the wrath of the Judge who had decided they did not deserve Addy although Andrew was her biological father; none of it seemed fair and she was behind it all. She could not dwell on the wrong but must concentrate on the right. How was she going to handle the situation with Andrew when he told her they were coming for Addy? She could only hope for some strange reason he would decide to let it slide tonight and she would leave in the morning.

He was in bed. She knew the stress had thrown Andrew and after he talked to Harper, or perhaps while talking to Harper he had laid on the bed and without meaning to fallen asleep. She slipped the phone from his hand and listened to the dial tone. All the while she prepared for bed her mind was making mental notes of what was needed. Most of all she had to think how much money she needed. She left her phone in the kitchen, rather than be tempted to use it.

She could not sleep, her mind was too active. Andrew awoke after midnight and pulled her to his side. "I missed you," he said. "I think I went to sleep talking to Harper. He'll never let me forget that." She turned into his arms. "I love you," he said. She knew their love had to be strong enough to last through this trial. She had never loved him more. "Sometimes we do strange things because we love," she said. "I know," he replied.

They were rushed the next morning, having overslept. "I'll be home during lunch," he said. "I need to talk to you about something. I've got to kiss the kids and go, now." Returning from their rooms, he pulled her close; their eyes did not stray from each other's face. "Never change," he said, tilting her chin, his lips against hers. "It took a while but what we've got is what every man longs for, I love you, Anne."

* * * * * *

When Andrew left, Anne called Ellen. "Ellen," she said in very hoarse voice. "I know Jewel is still with you, would there be a way you could go in to help Dr. Lonzo today, I cannot. Oh, thank you."

Two pillows in the floor board, a blanket in between car seats, and the little blue car was stuffed to the brim. She couldn't take the Suburban; it was what Andrew drove, besides it would be more noticeable. She adjusted the car seat belts, placed her jacket on top of the blanket, kissed each child and got behind the steering wheel. It was a short drive to pass by Harriet's home and equal time to Dr. Lonzo's. He came from the garage and motioned for her to drive inside where he quickly shut the door. "Open the trunk," he said. She did, supposing he would place Little Momma's suitcase inside but he was taking out what she had packed, from her blue car and placing in the gray one. Putting a finger to his lips he bade her be silent. He pointed to the emblem on the car; it was new to her and pointed to the license plate. Raising the compartment beneath the trunk protector he showed her first a newer tool box with a few necessary tools and then an old battered box which he opened. Beneath the tray he lifted that held kids toys, was a package containing bills of various denomination. He heard her gasp, and patted her shoulder as he whispered, "it's all right. Now let's put the baby's seats inside and exchange keys." He smiled, proud of all he accomplished. And last," he said, "the phones. Did you leave yours?" She nodded.

He showed her four phones. "One for Momma, one for you, one for Andrew and one for me; is your house key on here?" He was examining the key ring. "Where should I leave the phone?"

Anne sit down and wrote Andrew a note. *"Darling, remember your words, for the first time we have something, let us help each other to keep the faith. I love you, Andrew."* She hand the note to Dr. Lonzo. Put it and the phone under the pillow on the right hand side of the bed." She hugged him and said, "Thank you."

Leaving town they headed east. "Where are we going, Little Momma?" Anne felt a knot in her stomach and her heart ached but she was intent on putting as much distance between her sweet little Addy and Summer's mother as possible. Andrew was a lawyer, this might prove to be his biggest challenge in life but she trust he could do it, God willing, and she would face whatever was handed to her. For now, she and Olivia would do what they must to give him time to work his magic.

Olivia was studying the map, upside down. *We are headed this direction, she mumbled, yes, yes, we are on track, keep going. I tell you when to turn.* Olivia ran her fingers through her new haircut. "You like? Doctor and I had much fun cutting away that long black hair. I told him cut all over head about two inches long then I turn it red…auburn the box said. We love it. Doctor says I look ten years younger." She laughed. "Funny man, my doctor."

"You do look younger, but I can't imagine you cutting off all that beautiful hair."

"We give it to make a wig for cancer children." She smiled. "Worthwhile, don't you think?" Little Momma turned to check on children. "Do they sleep long as car goes down highway?"

"Yes, just about and heaven help us when they wake up. Tonight we will need a room with space for them to play."

"No worry, Doctor rented a suite. His friend did, anyway, and doctor paid him, just as mysterious car appeared in garage overnight and doctor's clandestine meeting which gave us phones and new id's and who knows what else…doctor felt like gangbusters and Perry Mason all together. He so proud."

Anne reached across to squeeze Olivia's hand. "I love both of you. You are so giving and loving to me."

"You are ours. We decided long ago, but it your decision whether we are yours."

"You are. I just never want to take you for granted nor abuse that love. I've never been loved that way before. Thank you."

CHAPTER 8

It was lunch hour. Ellen yawned. Anne's job was more than she had told them. Dr. Lonzo counted on her completely. She kept personal notes in her own little book that might help the doctor along with the forms she submitted for insurance purposes. It was a fast paced morning and now she found herself hungry.

"Come with me," Doctor Lonzo motioned to her, carrying two sacks he led the way to a small table in a screened area. "May I take you into confidence over our Anne?" He saw surprise register in her eyes as the question formed in her mind. He handed her a bottle of orange juice and a sandwich.

"Anne isn't sick?"

"No, our Anne is not sick. I tell you quickly what has happened. Today, Andrew is telling her if she were there that Family Services was coming to take Addy from them because Mrs. Walden had decided she wants custody of baby. Anne made up mind to run away. Olivia went with her. You must not tell this."

"Why would she run away?"

"To give Andrew time to correct Judges mistake. She overheard Andrew tell his friend. Now eat." He smiled. "And you cannot tell this to anyone. Eventually Andrew will probably tell you...he does not know yet, that she has run away. She will call him in time."

"It takes your appetite, doesn't it? "Ellen picked up the ham and cheese sandwich and laid it back down to slice in half. "Won't there be retribution for running away, maybe even jail time?"

"What would you do if someone came after your baby?" Dr. Lonzo laid down his sandwich and waited for her reply. "Andrew and Anne are not dealing with a Judge who is fair; he is Mrs. Walden's friend."

"Once someone did and I thought I would die. Should it happen again, I would defend her with my life."

"Tell me then, has she done wrong? Is there in the Bible an example we can turn to, to understand this? Has our Anne committed a sin or broke the law, how would the Creator look on this?"

"Truthfully, I do not know. There's no drug problem here, Anne and Andrew are good parents. I can't think of a single incident in the Bible that speaks of anything remotely related to this."

"Good. Our Annie had no way of knowing. She and her children are merely away on vacation."

Ellen saw him glance at the other half of her sandwich. "Dr. Lonzo would you like the rest of this sandwich?"

He laughed. "You caught me, didn't you? Yes, I would. Normally I have cereal and fruit for breakfast but today I overslept due to my clandestine night and I am hungry. Thank you Ellen and may I ask has it been hard on you this morning? If not, would you consider working until Anne returns, you have done a marvelous job."

* * * * * *

Dan arrived home before Ellen. Going down the hall he heard Ruthie reading to the younger twins and Jewel, as usual, working with Sammy and Danny at the portable black boards. "They know how to write their first names, Mr. Gates." She smiled, proud of her students. "They can count to twenty five and know all their colors and shapes."

"That's great, boys. Be sure to tell Miss Jewel thank you for teaching you." To Jewel he said, "You are doing a good job, Jewel. We are going to miss you." He noticed a pained expression came over her face. "Is there something wrong?"

"No, Sir, I just need a job longer than the month, I've put in applications but no one wants to hire me." For a moment she glanced down at the floor, "But Mr. Gates, I need employment to be able to pay for my wedding, otherwise it will be stand in front of the judge and that's it."

"There's nothing wrong with that, Jewel, what had you planned?"

"Well, Sir, I've made my dress, except for hemming it and I don't think I need a white dress to stand before a Judge, do you?"

Unaware to Jewel and Daniel, Ellen had come in and was standing in the hall beyond the door listening. "Daniel?" The boys came running, calling Momma, nearly knocking Daniel out of the doorway where he stood. Ellen was hugging her boys, kissing their cheeks and enjoying seeing them. "I need to talk to Daddy, can you finish your lessons with Jewel and then we'll have dinner."

"Are you all right?" Her smile calmed the alarm he'd felt when she said she needed to talk to him. They embraced and he walked with her back to the kitchen. Taking his hand she led him on out to the garden. "What's going on?"

"Have you heard from Andrew, today?" He shook his head, puzzled. "Let me tell you what has happened but you can't let on like you know to anyone. If Andrew decides to tell you, still don't tell him you know." She waited for her words to soak in and Daniel's nod of agreement. "Okay?" He nodded. "Here's how I understand it. Andrew arrived home yesterday, upset, and talked to Harper. Anne happened to come home and hear it and didn't tell him her instant plan. I say instant because she made a decision immediately and stuck with her plan."

"What in the world are you talking about? It almost scares me. Did she leave Andrew? What about the kids?"

"She did leave Andrew but not for the reason most women leave their husbands. She overheard him tell Harper Judge Springer told him Mrs. Walden wants Adeline and the Judge is going to push it through. He also said Andrew has to pay child support."

"What? That's incredible. Why would Anne leave, I don't understand…and Andrew is Addy's daddy."

"Andrew thinks after this weekend, the Judge will have Family Service come for Adeline."

"Who told this to you?"

"Doctor Lonzo," she spun around, her arms out, "Did you notice I'm wearing scrubs? And get this, Doctor Lonzo asked me if I'd stay on as his nurse until Anne returns."

"Babe?"

"I know, but I really need to work some to stay informed and it wasn't so bad because Anne keeps a book you can refer to on their patients, nothing that breaks their right to privacy but little things she needs to remember and it was very helpful to me." She pat his arm. "Unlike other doctors, Dr. *Lonzo* closes at three in the afternoon, then he makes rounds for an hour. That means I would go in at nine and be home by three thirty. Six hours on my feet, not hospital twelve hour shifts."

"And you are thinking, while Jewel is here…right?" Studying the situation, he finally said, "She just told me she needs to stay on, to make money for the wedding and I suspect their new beginning."

"I believe she and Ruthie can handle the twins and I'll listen to her with Ruthie's home schooling and see if she can do it and if she can I'll be helping both Anne and Dr. Lonzo. He's interesting to work with."

"Shouldn't he retire?"

"He has such fun and his patients love him. He slips into the language of the old country, often."

"Just don't you get to loving him?" Daniel pulled her into his arms, kissing her. "I'd be jealous."

"Lord help us, he's ancient." They laughed, Daniel nodding. "A reason he should retire?"

"We'll bring this up at dinner," Daniel said, "but you and I will have to spend more time with the kids."

Later at the dinner table, Ruthie had that peculiar look, "Momma, did you know you are going to work?"

"Really?" Ellen glanced at Dan and then Ruthie. "What makes you think that?"

Ruthie giggled. "Jewel's going to teach my home schooling and together we will watch the twins."

"Would you be up to that, Jewel?" Surprised, Jewel let her eyes roam around the table.

"Is this for real?" Everyone laughed and all together said, "Yes."

"Is that all, Ruthie?" Her mother held her attention. "Come on, why so reluctant?"

"It's the man in the blue shirt, Momma, and I'm pretty sure it's Evan."

"Ruthie, you have been seeing the man in the blue shirt often, why?"

"I think because he is sad. Is Evan sad, Jewel?"

"Yes, he is and I don't know why. He doesn't talk a lot but when he does I listen, but he hasn't talked about his family or why they have never associated with others. He was allowed to attend school but never have friends home, but I wasn't either, so I don't know if that is why he's quiet or not."

"But Jewel, I don't think Evan has parents or brothers or sisters. That's why I think I keep seeing him and he's worried whether you will be happy with him." Ruthie was deeply concerned over Evan. "You need to talk to him."

"I can't Ruthie. I told you, I can talk to you but it isn't easy talking to someone else," Jewel glanced at Ellen. "I'm sorry Miss Ellen; you all have done everything to make me feel welcome. I talked to Mr. Gates a while ago and if I make myself believe I'm going to be a teacher I can do it and I did that but otherwise I think like Evan I could go through life just listening; maybe that's why Evan and I are drawn to each other. We understand the kind of life we've been brought up in."

"Then you should be able to talk about anything if you are getting married to each other."

"Shouldn't he have his private thoughts? I don't want to intrude, in time I'll know."

"What about when you sing or play the piano?" Ellen was perplexed. "I didn't realize all this. The two of you performed so well, no one would know."

"It's because we both are trying so hard to put our upbringing behind us. Maybe we are doing all right because we have talked about this. I have told Evan my parents almost follow the old Quaker way to the rule and although he hasn't said, either his parents were missing out of his life or there were strong restrictions and I don't know why. Ruthie has brought me this far. Age doesn't matter with Ruthie."

"Momma? Can you talk to Jewel about being married? When I see Evan I feel he is afraid because he has never been around people too much and he's afraid that he will disappoint her. He writes songs about her because he's afraid." Ruthie turned to Ellen. "Momma, is this important or a small thing. I'm not old enough to know."

"I know, Sweetums, God has blessed and give you understanding beyond your years, but I understand this has confused you."

"It's different than usual," Ruthie agreed. "I haven't known what to do with it. Does God want me to know things like this?"

Ellen pulled her into her arms and kissed her on the forehead. Ruthie looked like any little girl, her hair tousled and the dust cloth in her hand but her eyes were troubled. Usually what she received was more a healing process but then maybe this was important to Jewel and Evan and needed a different kind of healing. Ruthie was troubled because Evan kept coming up in her mind and she had no answers.

* * * * * *

He found her standing in front of the closet; the radio was on, her favorite music playing. "Penney for your thoughts," Daniel slipped behind her, his arms around her waist, his head on her shoulder. "Do you have any idea how worried I get when you become quiet. I never know if you are thinking or too tired to think."

Ellen turned putting her arms around his neck, her gaze sweet and understanding. "Do you know I love you more every day? How could you be so considerate when you carry such a load every work week and help your aunt to run her business, too?" She grinned, "Then come home to a houseful of children?"

"Are you all right?" His dark eyes would not leave her face until she answered. "When I remember you were in stage four cancer and didn't want anyone to know the full extent because they might focus on you rather than Bitty or Marigold who were sick during the same time, I don't want this family to go through that again and if it means I must stay alert to how you are every day, then I will."

"Daniel," she chided, "I appreciate all your concern but if you don't loosen up you will have health issues. I was actually thinking about Jewel and Evan. They've not had a regular date and yet they plan to be married. They haven't kissed because they are bashful and always being in front of our children or the people at church, that isn't going to happen."

"What are you planning," he teased, "a secret rendezvous where they let their silent inexperienced hearts run wild?" He led her through a simple dance routine as they talked, the song on the radio one they had listened to while dating. "You know, Mrs. Gates, you were quite the restricted young woman for dating, I might say, I thought you were never going to let me kiss you and I so wanted to."

"And once you kissed me…." She laid her head on his shoulder. "We had the most wonderful courtship, it had to be …because I had promised myself to never look at another man and certainly never entertain the thought of marrying again. But you wore me down with your love for me and Ruthie. I can't imagine if I had let you pass by but I was afraid I could never live up to your lifestyle. I was a struggling nurse."

"From the moment I saw you in the shoe store, I knew I would never give up until you were my wife." The music ended and Daniel pulled her close. "Now, back to the original subject…you were thinking about Jewel and Evan but what exactly did you have in mind?" Suddenly he chuckled and she gave him a puzzled look. "You worried about my lifestyle and yet, I have pinned you down to being mommy of the year with two sets of twins and our sweet Ruthie. But back to Jewel and Evan, what about them?"

"They should be courting, don't you agree? With many young people going into marriage with the idea if it doesn't work they can divorce and find someone else, I don't want to see Jewel and Evan experiencing that scenario, how can we encourage them to plan a weekly date, just the two of them to learn how time will be when they are alone?" She sit on the edge of the bed and Daniel joined her.

"If the rains had let up and the workers could do their job, the bridge to Evan's property and Jewel's folks would be in and they would already have left us." He lay back on the bed. "Let's think on this and I was wondering what Haley had to say, I was checking the calls and saw her name."

"When did she call? I didn't know. I haven't seen her since we three met at Milliee's."

"Maybe it's not important; she only called once according to the listings." His thoughts were fired up now. "I don't suppose you've heard from Anne either? Andrew is thinking they need another lawyer on the case, fearful I believe that he might overlook something and as he said, "you only get one chance,"

"How true, one chance at so many things; this is the longest since Anne and I became friends that we haven't talked or at least found time to have a cup of coffee together. But filling in her place with Dr. Lonzo, I am busy and I'll have to admit, I may be tired but I enjoy his company. He truly cares about his patients."

"Just don't let it wear you down," Daniel cautioned. "If you need me and I don't answer the phone tomorrow I promised Aunt Georgia we would work on Hutson's next Ball."

"Our lives began with Hutson's Ball, my first glance at how the wealthy live." She laughed. "They get up and put their clothes on each morning just like everyone else, they have problems, they have family and faith just like the poor. Where did people start the tale that each category of what a person has makes us different?"

"Before the cross when Mary anointed Jesus before he was crucified and the disciples thought it a waste of money, meaning the ointment could have been sold and the money given to the poor, Jesus said, "The poor you will have always with you but what Mary has done will be remembered through time."

"Then, the rich also are present in society, the one who claimed Jesus body was rich and a believer."

"Praise the Lord," Daniel said. "God had it worked out every step of the way, for his beloved Son and so he has our life's plan also; which means, we've skirted all around the subject of Jewel and Evan." He chuckled, "Isn't it safe to say, God will work out their plan to marry and they'll figure it out on their own?"

"Now that that's settled," Ellen quipped, "I shall rise and go meddle in Haley's business. Whatta you think Daddy of the year?"

She leaned down to kiss him, knowing he would try to pull her beside him. "Wherever we fit in the categories, we are blessed in the single fact we have each other."

"Amen." Daniel agreed and they laughed together. "God be with us and all His children."

* * * * * *

Ellen dialed Haley's number. "Hey."

"Daniel saw your name in the directory. Did you call? I'm working this week and missed you, all together."

"I'm at Mom and Dad's," Haley informed her. "Jeremy's with me but I'd like to see you and Marigold tomorrow if there's a chance you can meet me." Quiet for a minute, she added, "It just hit me you said you are working. That takes care of noon hour, doesn't it?"

"How about around three thirty?"

"Where?"

"How about the Little Tea Garden on Main? There are several outdoor tables with privacy."

"If you don't hear back from me, that means Marigold can make it. See you there." Haley hung up.

* * * * * *

Ellen arrived home to pull into the drive ahead of Daniel. Once they were inside the garage, the two climbed out to meet each other and embrace. "What's going on down the road," Daniel took her hand to lead her out to the curb where they stood staring down the street where two moving vans were trying to back into the drive.

"Looks like our neighbors are moving in. Look at that lawn they laid and the landscaping. Wow."

"Nothing beats yours," Ellen had her arm looped through his and still managed a kiss on his cheek. "But it is pretty. They must have a lawn boy to help with it; didn't you tell me they are all three senior citizens?"

"I've only seen them hurrying around, nothing up close and personal. It does appear three women."

"That's nice they get around good." She thought of Dr. Lonzo's patients. Arthritis, bad knees, weak back were the reasons they came to see him and all seemed to put a great trust in him. "I know I'll be ready to stay home with the children when Anne gets back, but it has been an eye opener working at the clinic." She yawned and Daniel turned toward the house. "Don't guess you've heard from Andrew?"

"Well, yes, I have. The first time was when he realized Anne really wasn't coming home the next day. He was angry, no, he was mad, fuming mad but then the next day when he called he was sad, if she hadn't left, he said, the Judge had it set up to pick up Addy and him and Anne be damned, are the words he used, he said the judge is that ruthless."

"So does he hear from Anne daily?" They entered the house by way of the sun room, "What about Andrew has he found a loop hole, yet?" She saw the girls had made tea. "Is he mad at Anne?"

"No, but his anger is driving him to work harder at what lies ahead of them. The Judge ask him if her leaving was planned and he said he could honestly say he had no idea at all." He watched Ellen lift the lid off the cooker. She had told Ruthie and Jewel to sit the cooker on the sun porch, and turn it to medium. She had a roast with potatoes, carrots and green beans on the side lined up for supper. He smiled seeing the roast. Evidently he planned for more than family. "How long until we eat, Babe?"

"I'd say thirty minutes. I have to make tea, warm the bread and tell the girls to wash up the twins."

"What do you say I give Andrew a quick call and ask him and Evan over?"

"That would be nice. I'll tell the girls. They will be coming in to sit the table." She listened as Dan made the call. From what she heard, the two either had to cook or eat out, the invitation was well received.

"They'll be right over. Shall I sit the table and get the extra chairs. That way we can talk."

"I just want to hear about our brave Anne. My goodness, she has changed. I love it."

"She was pretty timid when I met her." Dan kind of nodded his head. "In those days, Andrew had beaten her down I guess you'd say broke her spirit and then you got hold of her and we saw her self-esteem come back. But now she expects Andrew to carry his own weight as long as she is working. This is his entire story if you believe him."

"I believe him," Ellen replied, "and I can hardly stand to think they'd divorce but there's conflict right now." She drew a deep breath. "How can they stand to disagree or fight when they're apart?"

"It seems they aren't really fighting but they are disagreeing about her taking Addie away. He's afraid the court will bear down on him and Anne, thinking they knew they were going to be served and Anne said she wasn't taking the chance of Addie being taken away and going through suffering that will affect her into her adult life." He paused to count the forks in his hand. "What do you think?"

"I wish she was here, but think how warped Mrs. Walden's daughter was, that's probably what stays in Anne's mind, the fact Summer was in to so much and her mother ignored her daughter completely, now her mother wants to raise Addie."

"When you put it that way," Daniel said, "I'm with Anne. Summer was messed up pretty badly."

"Hey, they're knocking. Our friends come in a hollering." Dan was racing to open the door. "Come on in, we're just minutes to our evening meal. What do you guys want to drink? Tea, water, diet coke, right, Hon?"

Ellen was on her way to call the kids, hugging the two as she passed by. "Ellen looks good," Andrew said. "Here's a little gift for her helping us all the time. I was with Anne when she got it."

"What are you doing in the mall?" Dan had to tease a little. "Bet he was having a manicure." He winked at Evan. "Come on Brother, a little teasing makes the heart stronger. It's part of the fun of life." The thunder of feet coming down the hall saved Andrew answering. Dan saw his austere expression.

Ruthie and Jewel were carrying the younger twins to sit them in high chairs, while Dan pushed Sammy and Danny closer to the table. Andrew watched with an almost longing in his eyes. "You miss Andy and Addie, don't you?" Ellen was back, sitting the bread center of the table. Leaning down she kissed Andrew's cheek. "I can identify with that. When Ruthie was missing I thought I would die, but I kept hope." She leaned back waiting for his reply. "Tell me, do you have hope?"

"I have hope this will all turn out right, Ellen, but without Anne here by my side I have more fear."

"Do you have any idea about Anne's going away at this time, if it will be used against you?"

"I'm sure our attorney will counter with the fact the grandmother never ask to see her grandchild while her own daughter was alive."

"They will ask why?" Ellen took the seat next to Daniel. "Do you know the answer?"

"According to her friends, Summer refused her because while she was growing up her mother was never there for her nor believed what was happening to her." With the children seated he grew quiet.

"Let us bless the food." Daniel prayed, "Father we thank you for your presence and for our friends, Evan and Andrew joining us, now Lord we ask your blessing on the food for our bodies. We give thanks for the blessings you give to us, for Ellen and the girls taking care of our meal and we ask your blessing on those with need that someone will bring an answer and comfort to them. In your gracious name we pray. Amen.

"How are you today, Evan?" Ellen asked. "Have you had a busy day?"

"I've changed the oil in Miss Harriet's car and tried to service it for use." He examined his hands. "I really had to scrub my hands, Miss Ellen, I was concerned what I got on them might not come off."

Daniel gave Ellen a knowing smile. "I told you Harriet would probably offer the use of her car. Andrew's used it and Anne. The list goes on and on and that car holds up like the gem it is." He grinned. "Is it large enough to suit you, Evan?"

"Yes Sir, it is. But when you're walking you're grateful to have something to get around in. I thanked Miss Harriet."

He sought Jewel, sitting between the older twins and smiled, satisfied now they could ride in their own vehicle places. "Jewel, tell them what Miss Harriet suggested."

"She said we should ride down by the river, there's a gazebo and couples getting married carve their name on a special board the city has put up and that we should too."

Jewel blushed as everyone at the table clapped their hands while Jewel took very small helpings of food, she was too embarrassed to eat and Evan kept his eyes on her and when everyone was finished the men pushed their chairs back from the table so the young couple would understand it was all right for them to leave, still Jewel looked to Ellen to help her clear the table, but Ellen said, "Go on with Evan, Jewel, and have a sweet evening together."

"My goodness," Daniel managed to say quietly, "I have worried about those two not knowing each other well enough to be married but I believe they are so compatible nothing much matters. Like Ellen, I've finally decided they will be all right."

"That's the most I've heard Evan say," Andrew replied. It was then his phone rang and a smile lit up his face. "It's Anne." He glanced around to be sure the children had left the room and answered the phone. "Anne, are you all right?" They couldn't hear her reply. "I miss you, too, Babe, but since you're away from here, maybe we needed the children out of the reach of Springer's goons. I'm trying hard Anne but I don't know anything, yet." In a minute's time, there were tears running down Andrew's cheeks, "I know, Son, Daddy misses you, too, you just take care of Momma and Sissy and I'll see you soon." The line went dead and Andrew collapsed in his chair.

"Ellen, get Ruthie and let's lay hands on Andrew and pray. Tell the boys Daddy said stay in their rooms."

Ruthie joined her parents and the three placed their hands on Andrew as he sit at the table. "Father, God," Daniel began. "We are sad when our brother has such serious concerns and Lord we bring those concerns to you now. Your scripture says where two or more are joined together in prayer, you hear, and if we come to you, you hear us and we have not because we ask not, but tonight Lord, we are asking that you strengthen the hope in Andrew's heart, Addy is his child and she is the one we bring to you now and ask you to be ever present with Anne as she watches over the children. Keep them all safe, Lord. We thank you that Little Momma is with them. We don't know what is needed but Andrew is our friend and the matters of his heart, those he holds dear are our concerns. Lord, we know Andrew and Anne will raise Addy in the presence of your son and as his friends we will support and be there for them. Help us Lord to trust you, and to be able to say thy will be done. We praise you Lord for the lives of our friends and the love they have for you and each other, comfort them as only you are able and give them joy that comes only from you as we ask this all in your gracious Holy name." Everyone said, "amen."

"Sometimes, Brother, all we can do is pray. Our hands are tied on a worldly scale but our Lord is a mighty God that can move mountains and raise up springs in the desert, truly it is in His hands." Daniel hugged Andrew as Andrew tried to keep tears from forming.. Ruthie took his hand and held it, looking into his eyes, her gaze did not stray. After a time, she leaned forward to kiss his cheek and went back to her room.

"I can hardly bear to tell you this," Andrew said. "Today, I received an anonymous call from the building where Judge Springer keeps his office. The voice told me it is not that Mrs. Walden wants Addy, one of her friends is unable to bear a child and she plans to give Addy to that friend. That's why my heart is so heavy and at this time I cannot tell Anne." The pain aged Andrew's appearance. "That is the worst scenario I can imagined, our Addy given to a stranger when I'm her biological father."

"I cannot imagine your thoughts," Daniel replied, "but Ellen's situation was once so near what you describe," he called to Ellen in the kitchen. "It was a terrible ordeal, wasn't it?"

Wiping her hands on a dish towel, Ellen came to sit in the chair next to Andrew. "I was just getting clean glasses in case we needed them. I don't know if you remember, Ruthie's daddy decided if we couldn't raise five hundred thousand dollars, he would file for custody of Ruthie and move her to Florida where I could not see her. We don't know if he could have won but it was the worry, what if he did." She sighed, heavily, in remembering. "All we could do was trust the Lord. I practically stayed on my knees and Dan was there for me. I'm sorry Anne felt she must leave, but from what you said, I believe you now agree."

Andrew nodded. "After the call, I began to see how Mrs. Walden's mind works. She is almost as cold and hardened as her husband. Clayton never cared how a situation affected another person as long as he got what he wanted, now I wonder, did he learn that from her? She was the one with wealth, he was as poor as me when he started out, but he did have a grandmother who delved in witch craft, perhaps the devil has more strength than we realize if one sells their soul to him and Clayton boldly stated he did."

"There's a scripture that says we as Christians wrestle not against flesh and blood but against principalities, against powers, against the rulers of the darkness of this world. It's found in Ephesians, and I believe it." Ellen's thoughts turned to tomorrow; what would Haley have to tell them? Why was the devil attacking their friends? She knew when her and Dan's lives were turned upside down, their friends had kept them lifted in prayer and that was not what the devil wanted at all.

"We can't let our faith falter and yet, even the disciple's faith waned at times, but our world has become too lenient in areas of life that used to be black and white as to our decision what we should do; now there are shades of gray or no shade at all, if you understand what I'm saying. What will our Lord say to us, when we accept those things he has warned us we must not?"

"Is it the same for everyone?" Andrew asked. "What exactly do you have in mind, Daniel?"

"Well, an example might be, God said Honor the Sabbath and keep it Holy but we've become lax on that and many others."

"I was the world's worst fool," Andrew admitted. "I committed adultery. I quit church. My business ethics became more a race to succeed at any cost than run the race with integrity. Like Paul the apostle, if I hadn't met the Lord, and I believe I had met Him when

I was a child, it was on that dirty bathroom floor with Harper's hand on my back praying for me when Andy almost died He became my Savior."

"Hallelujah, Brother." Daniel smiled. "If you had hope there, and the Lord blessed you, can't he bless you again? I don't know his plan, Andrew, but I know if you have to go through the fire, he'll be there."

CHAPTER 9

THE LITTLE TEA GARDEN

Leaving Dr. Lonzo's office, Ellen checked the room where the two women spent their days. "Come with me," she said, motioning toward the door. With the key in her hand she waited for them to shuffle past. "I won't be here tomorrow." She was almost certain they understood because a look passed between them. Locking the door, she hurried to the locker where she kept her purse and jacket each day. She had done it again, left her purse open, but no one was in the back of the office except Doctor Lonzo.

Marigold and Haley were seated in a protected corner of the garden. "The wind's picking up," Marigold said in greeting. "We thought we should find a sheltered spot. How are you?"

Pecking a kiss on their cheeks, they waited for her to be seated as Haley pointed to a glass of tea. "Marigold thought Raspberry was your favorite." Ellen smiled and nodded. There were a few minutes of getting settled and then Marigold and Ellen looked expectantly to Haley.

Picking up the paper she had peeled from her straw, Haley, folded it, unfolded and folded it again. "I don't know where to start." Her eyes had turned sad as she stared at the two of them. "I don't know what to do. You know the circumstance." She glanced down to her lap, turning loose of the paper and twisting her hands together under the table. "How do I say this?" Her bottom lip quivered and she was about to cry. "I...."

Marigold reached across the table and patted for Haley to bring up her hands, taking them in to her own. "Haley, are you pregnant?" Ellen's hand stacked on top of Marigold's as they waited for her reply.

Haley nodded, the tears spilling from her eyes to run down her cheeks. "Yes."

"What do you want to do, Haley?"

"If Jeremy suspected his father did anything to me," her breath caught as her shoulders shook. "I don't know if he would hate me or his father for not telling him, either way it's not good, but this isn't something I can pursue…I mean," again a deep breath made her shudder, "I can't find out if its Jeremy's. How can I do this? And then there's his mother to consider, what she would think of me."

"You really feel Jeremy would not handle it well?" Haley's gaze lifting to Ellen, gave her the answer. "Then, what have you decided? Now, before Jeremy knows, what do you feel you must do?"

"Ellen," Haley's voice was distraught. "You would never allow me to abort a baby. How could I? It's against God's laws." Now her crying became great sobs that wracked her body. "What can I do, Ellen?"

"This is not my decision, Haley. I don't know the trauma of your thoughts, your very soul, but I know you have the answer within you. I'm speaking as a Nurse now. I have to allow you a privilege that I as a Christian might answer differently."

"I've not entertained aborting a baby that could be Jeremy's, who I love dearly but if it were his father's." Her sob deepened, "That's where the pain comes in. I want it to be my husbands." She laid her head on the table and sobbed, her shoulders shaking, as Marigold and Ellen gripped her arms.

"We have to get out of here," Marigold whispered, "The place is beginning to fill up."

"Let's go," Ellen said, standing, "Put Haley between us and walk out as though she is sick. She is." Once on the outside, Ellen said, "Get in my vehicle. We will come back. Dr. Lonzo gave me a key to his office and there's no one there." Marigold climbed into the back with Haley and Ellen drove the short distance.

It was while searching her purse for the key; Ellen discovered her wallet was missing. "I can't believe I've lost my wallet, but it's not here." She unlocked the door and they went in. "This way," she said, leading toward the small room where she and Dr. Lonzo ate their lunch. She opened the door and there sat the two women who slept on the table in one of Dr. Lonzo's waiting rooms each day and in their arms, each held a young child.

"How did you get in?" Ellen's voice was sharp with surprise. The older of the two arose from the chair and came to Ellen holding out Ellen's wallet. The other cowered, trying to hide her baby in the folds of her garment.

"We meant no harm," the one said. "We are without means to purchase room or food."

"Do you stay here every night?"

"Only those nights you leave purse where we find key to open side door."

"This is getting scary, Ellen." Marigold and Haley had come and were clutching each other's arms.

"Are there others?" Ellen asked.

"No, we have no one. Our husbands have either abandoned us or been taken by your police."

"What have you done with your babies while you slept in the room on the table?"

The one standing motioned Ellen should follow, leading to the room they occupied by day. Beneath the table they slept on was a set of two sliding doors. She opened one, inside several of the blankets used in the office as needed had been folded to make a pallet of sorts and on the side a meager supply of baby items.

"The babies have been here all along?" The woman nodded. "Why have your babies not cried?"

"Our babies do not cry."

"I'm not sure I understand that but you cannot stay here." Sadness enveloped the woman's face.

"We have nowhere to go." Ellen seemed to study the woman, momentarily and made a decision.

She opened her wallet. "Have you taken anything?" The woman shook her head. "Then what I have I will give you. A block down the street there's a motel." She counted out three twenty dollar bills.

"Don't let them charge you more than this as a total for tonight's stay." She then gave her the last twenty. "This will buy food and I will check with you tomorrow. Do you understand?" The woman nodded.

When the two left with their babies, Marigold took a deep breath and sank on to one of the vacant chairs. "Do we need to case the joint?" Haley stared at her. "You know, in case there's more."

"How do you know what to do, Ellen?" Haley was in awe. "You didn't hesitate. Is that part of being a Christian or a nurse?"

For the first time, Ellen chuckled. "I think it was nervous energy or adrenalin, I was as shocked as you, but what can you do? We can't have the Police here, they'd call Dr. Lonzo and how do we know he wouldn't get excited and one thing lead to another and he'd mention Anne. I'll tell him tomorrow. Now let's get back to you, Haley. What, in your sanest moment, have you thought of doing?"

"I'm scared to death, Ellen. So much is riding on this. I can't abort this baby, no matter who's the father. I think I'm willing to take the chance no one will ever have to know outside of the three of us and I know Jeremy will fall in love with the baby." Tears threatened to start again, but she blinked them back. "The thing I worry about most is having to be around Jonathan Southern but if Jeremy's dad truly is unaware of what he does, then, maybe I'll never have that worry. Will you stand with me?"

"When did you decide this, Haley?" Marigold was puzzled. "At the Tea Garden you didn't have any answers."

"When Ellen made the decisions concerning those women, I decided I had to deal with this situation. I will love this baby and fight to the death of me to keep its beginning sacred regardless of the action that conceived it and I will not cease to pray this is Jeremy's baby."

The three hugged. "What an evening," Marigold quipped. "It's almost unbelievable."

* * * * * * *

Andrew was in the kitchen staring into the refrigerator when the doorbell rang. "I hope it is someone bearing food," he muttered, stepping quickly through the rooms. He opened the door to find a policeman standing there.

"Mr. Graves," he handed over a sheaf of papers. "Sir, you have been served." Andrew did not answer nor seem to hear the comment. Instead, he took the papers to the kitchen, laid them on the counter top and finished what he had begun; trying to determine if there was anything to eat had become a problem.

"Life's pretty dull when you sink to this," he said aloud, scraping the peanut butter jar for enough to spread across a double thick slice of bread. This time the ringing of the phone interrupted his feeding. "Andrew?"

"HI, Babe, who else would it be?" He forgot the sandwich and listened to Anne on the other phone. "I need to see my boy. Can you come home, Anne? What's going on? Not much we've not seen before."

"We're doing all right. Addy loves the sand with her little bucket and scoop and Andy runs in the edge of the water, until the waves come in. He can't stand to be splashed." She laughed. "How are you, my love?"

"I'm lonesome." He was toying with the mail when he noticed it was from the court. "Anne." Surprise was in his voice. "Anne. I just answered the door. I wasn't paying attention. Anne, now I've been served papers by the court." He riffled through the papers quickly. "I thought it pertained to you but now it has my name on it and we are in contempt of court. If we do not present ourselves and Addy we could both spend time in jail." Despair was in Andrew's voice. "Judge Springer is after me, Anne."

She was quiet on the other end of the line. "You are a lawyer, Andrew. You are brilliant. Do your homework. I'm not bringing Addy home to give to some stranger with no blood connection."

"Anne, they will hunt you down. They have the money and means to do so."

"I love you Andrew. We've talked our limit on minutes. See what you can do. Bye."

* * * * * *

Andrew was restless. He left the house, aimlessly walking, or so he thought, until he ended up at Harriet's. Knocking on the door, waiting for Hattie, he was surprised when Harriet answered. Seeing Andrew, she smiled. "Come in here, you ragamuffin. How did you know I'm feeling lonely with our boy gone?"

"I guess because I'm lonely, myself." He followed her to her favorite sitting place the two matching yellow chairs. "Harriet, what are we going to do, Anne and I? The Judge wants to destroy me personally for Mrs. Walden's sake and Anne refuses to come home which leaves us in contempt of court. If we both have to go to jail, what happens to our children? They become wards of the court. I never in my wildest dreams could have concocted this tale."

They talked for two hours, going over the details. When Andrew left, she had comforted him by listening, fed him left overs and hugged his neck on the way out the door. When she was certain he was down the street, Harriet picked up the phone. "Are you free tomorrow, say around four in the evening? Good, I'll meet you at Becker Steel's first floor office."

"I declare," she said out loud, "I've never seen such a mess. There's Andrew and Anne, the new couple, Jewel and Evan, planning marriage showing little adoration for each other and my child…" She shuddered, "She is always in the thick of things. Thank goodness Dan and Ellen are on solid ground."

* * * * * *

Dan was on the phone. "Yes, come for lunch after church. If we don't get together, I'm afraid we will leave the Lord out of this Holy season. So much seems to happen each day of our week, we find ourselves wondering if we observed all seven days." He laughed at what was said by the other person. Fifteen times he made the call. "Whew, I'm glad the inviting is over, now we can plan the menu."

"Did you call anyone from Newhaven?"

"Do you think they would come?" He stopped what he was doing, his eyes resting on Ellen. "It's an hour's drive."

"How will we know if they aren't invited?"

"Hon, can you handle that many more with working five days this week?"

"Ruthie and Jewel said they would be sure the house is in order while watching the twins." She smiled. "I think filling in for Anne has been a vacation for me from washing and ironing and folding clothes, not to mention cooking and cleaning. You get my meaning Daddy of the year?"

Dan lay down the phone book where he had been searching for a number and crossed the room. "Uh, uh, uh, Momma of many, this calls for an old fashioned kiss for your sugar daddy." She was laughing as he pulled her close. Burying his face in her hair he said, "I still remember the first time I saw you in old Shu's shoe store. I made up my mind on first sight, "I'm going to marry that girl."

"Oh, you did, did you?" She pecked a kiss on his lips. "Did you also plan we'd have two sets of twins?"

"No," he gave her a real kiss. "Do you want to try for three sets?"

"No, sir, I'll pass on that presently, five chilun's suits me just fine."

"You can think about that tomorrow," he said. They were laughing. "I never knew love grew through the years. I guess I thought it would be so grand starting out that would be enough. We are blessed."

"You got that right, Big boy," she turned toward the laundry room. "I've got to teach these girls how to fold sheets." When she came through the next time, Daniel had an update.

"Add six adults and two toddlers." He grinned, "and Mable and her new husband may join us, too."

"I take it we get to see the new baby?" Dan nodded. "Ruthie will be so pleased to see all the Markels."

* * * * * *

Andrew sat by the phone waiting for Anne's call. "Hi, Babe, guess what? Dan and Ellen are having everyone over for Easter dinner after church. There's no evening service." He paused, "You've got time to drive home."

"No, Andrew. I miss you terribly and I know you miss the kids but I won't turn Addy over to her."

"I miss you Anne." He sounded so forlorn, she shut her eyes and stared at the ceiling. "Please, Anne."

"What if, Andrew, what if they put Addy in someone else's home and none of us knew what treatment she would receive? Can you really bear that? You're her daddy, for heaven's sakes."

"Can you miss Easter with us together and can you see us in prison for contempt of court and our children wards of the court?" He heard the click before the line went silent. "She will come home," he said to the empty house, "Oh, dear God, I pray Anne brings herself and our children home. Please." He was so troubled he went to bed, avoiding the refrigerator with its near empty peanut butter and stale bread.

He thought of the days when Anne would never have gone against him. She was like a scared little rabbit. Now she would move heaven and hell if possible for her children. In spite of himself, he grinned. She was quite a girl but if she didn't come home he was going to have to buy trousers a size smaller.

*   *   *   *   *   *   *

"Well, I'll have to say, this is nice. I don't think we've gone to bed together in two weeks. Has it been that long?" Jeremy propped up on one elbow, stared into Haley's face. "I've missed you, Miss Real Estate lady of the week. Isn't that what Mr. Dalton said when he called? Do they always call and congratulate their people, or are you the one made them take notice?"

"He did say very few sell three houses their first month." She smiled. "That was nice he called."

"Yeah," Jeremy ran circles on the material covering her stomach. "I like the feel of that. Is that satin?"

"Imitation I imagine." She lay a hand on his. "Can we turn off the lights?"

"Are you sleepy? It's early..." He searched the dresser for the clock. "Haley it's only nine. We're lucky if we get to bed by eleven these days."

"What are you doing down at the office?" She yawned, scooting into the hollow of his body. "I'm so tired."

His arm closed around her. "We're ordering parts for the busy season. Got to have what our customers need." His hand was flat on her stomach. "Are you all right? I feel a little rise, there." She didn't answer. He peeped around her shoulder. "Haley, Haley," he sang her name softly. "Are you asleep, already?"

She didn't answer. Disappointed he started to lay back. "Did you see the note I left on the counter? Dan and Ellen are having dinner at their house, Sunday. We might as well go since Mom and Dad are…" He sank back on the bed, pulling her closer. "I never dreamed my parents would file for divorce."

He awoke the next morning, hearing Haley in the bathroom, it sounded like…yes, she was sick. So that was what was wrong last night. He guessed he felt better. "You all right, Haley?" She didn't answer, he heard the toilet flush, water running and then she came back to fall onto the bed. She was pale and as he found her hand she was clammy too. "You really are sick, aren't you?"

* * * * * * *

"Yeah, sure, Ma," Marigold caught Matt's eyes. "It's your favorite mother in law," she said as much into the phone as to Matt. "He's sitting right there on the bed in his boxers looking as sexy as all get out." Marigold laughed. "Oh, Ma, you know you like it when I talk dirty." Her laughter became more boisterous, "So you don't have a boyfriend, well, I'll find you one." She turned full-faced to Matt, "Can you believe she said she didn't say any of that?" Marigold crossed to the bed and hand the phone to Matt. "You see if you can talk some sense to her. I know you have men working for you would be glad to date Harriet of Becker Iron and Steel works."

"Yes, Ma, I agree with you. I know you didn't say any of that." He winked at Marigold. "The kids are both asleep. Guess you got an invite to dinner at Dan and Ellen's Sunday? Yeah, we'll pick you up for church. I'll do my best. Goodnight, Ma." He hung up laughing. "She said I should do something about you."

He pat the space beside him as he lay back on the bed. "Come here, Tinkerbelle, I plan to follow your mother's orders." She came running across the floor and fell on him. "Well, I guess that's a start."

* * * * * *

Ellen found Dr. Lonzo sitting threading his fingers through his hair, elbows on the table. "You look worried. What's wrong?"

"Cleaning lady did not come last night. Commodes are smelly and nasty. Sinks need scrubbing. I, a doctor, must I clean floors and mop sinks?"

Ellen placed her hands out, palms up. "I am a nurse; do you want me to clean commodes and sinks and mop floors today? I know how. I guarantee you I know how to clean."

"No, No, No. I just don't know what to do without Little Momma. She always pull me out of problem."

A knock at the door drew their attention to the clock on the wall. "Ten minutes," Dr. Lonzo said.

The person knocking was persistent. Ellen opened the door. There stood the two ladies carrying their babies. "Your floor need cleaning," the one who spoke before had become the official speaker. Ellen was wondering how she knew. "Your toilet is dirty. I clean. You pay me. Yes?" She looked expectantly to the doctor. "I clean better than you ever see. Yes?" She held out her hand. "You pay?"

"Yes, we will pay you. Minimum wage, we need to see how good you are at cleaning. Supplies are in…"

"I know supplies." The spokesperson motioned her sister to follow, babies and all. "We clean," she said.

"Well, that was timely, wasn't it?" Ellen and Dr. Lonzo stared at each other. "Let's go to work, Doctor."

Throughout the morning she listened for an infant's cry but it never came. The bathrooms sparkled. At noon when the waiting room was vacant the floor became as new. "How do they do that?" Julie the receptionist whispered behind their backs. "I want them to come to my house."

"Have you heard a baby cry?" Ellen asked.

"Why should I, we haven't had any babies." Julie gave her a strange look. "That's a different doctor…"

"Follow me," Ellen said, taking her into the unused examining room where she opened the doors under the table. "What are those?"

Julie stared at two sleeping babies, wrapped round and snoozing away. Ellen closed the door quietly and motioned to be quiet as they made their exit.

Once outside the room, Julie whispered, "Can I have one?"

"No, those are taken. You have to get your own."

The clock on the wall sounded three thirty and Dr. Lonzo removed his white jacket to hang on the hook behind the door. He was smiling as he observed the clean floors in the rooms he could see through the open doors. "How you know those women could clean when you hire them, just like little Momma."

"I didn't know. I told them we'd see how good they are. If you are satisfied, we need money."

CHAPTER 10

uthie was in the garden. She and the older twins were pulling volunteer clover out of the day lilies. Sheltered from wind by the line of trees on three sides there were several varieties of flowers beginning to bloom in the garden. "Daddy, why are we pulling the clover? The flowers look like little round balls. I think they're pretty."

Daniel came to where the twins were stooped down looking intently at the plants. "What are they looking for?" He whispered. Ruthie pulled a clump of clover out to show him; in the clump was a four leaf clover. "I see, good job, Ruthie." He pat her on the back, smiling at her ingenuity. "That seems to keep them settled down, doesn't it?" He started away and turned back. "I came to tell you those are seeds and if we leave them, we'll have even more clover in the flower beds. They are pretty but they draw bees and we don't want you children stepping on the bees should you come barefoot in the garden."

"Are you going to work, Daddy?"

"I was waiting for Evan. He is going to paint the front post for me. We've had a lot of rain this winter and it's washed them out."

"I see him coming down the street," Ruthie pointed. "Does Jewel know he's coming?" Ruthie smiled. "She always has to comb her hair and take off that apron she wears when we clean house."

"You don't like aprons?" He teased her, pulling on her pony tail. "Maybe Jewel don't like pony tails."

"Our house is not that dusty, Daddy and Jewel won't put her hair up no matter how hot she gets."

"Is that a religious thing with Jewel?" Daniel stopped to consider. "I never heard that before."

"No, it's Jewel's Momma told her to always do that and never use a rubber band on her hair it would break it off." Ruthie's expression showed a lack of understanding. "Do you think her Momma will boss Evan, too?" Ruthie appeared almost frustrated.

"I don't think Evan would take to bossing," Daniel laughed. "Most of us men don't but we'll wait and see."

"Sometimes Jewel tells me things about her Momma and Daddy that makes me think they shouldn't live close to her parents."

"How old are you?" Daniel smiled and pulled her close. "You are thinking on big subjects to be so young."

"I don't know, daddy, sometimes I feel I'm supposed to, and other times I wish I didn't think so much. It's like I want everyone to like each other and get along, but I don't think Jewel's parents like Evan because they don't want her to leave them."

"Well, your Mom and I would miss you if you left us. You're not planning to soon, are you?"

"Oh, you're teasing me." Ruthie looked to where the boys were down on their knees digging something. "What is it?" She hurried down to find them starting to pull fur and twigs away form a hole in the ground. "Daddy?" She got his attention and motioned for him to come to where the boys were digging.

"What is it?" He and Evan had hurried. "Oh, boys, don't take out anymore. That's a rabbit's nest." The boys stepped back and Daniel stooped down, with a stick, he peeled away a layer of covering. "See. There. Baby bunnies. Their Momma has probably gone hunting for food. Aren't they little?"

"Can we hold them?" The boys ask together, as always, perfectly timed in rhythm with each other.

"No, Son. That's why I used a stick and not touch them. Their mother might not like it if we handle her babies."

"I wouldn't hurt them, Daddy. I just want to hold them."

"No son, they're not very old and they might die."

"They're going to eat Momma's flowers," Sammy said. "We better get them out."

"We could keep them in our bedroom," Danny agreed. "We could feed them."

"No, boys. Now don't even think about it. I'm going to work and I want those rabbits there when I return."

"Danny, they will have Momma's flowers eat by the time we eat our jelly worms."

"I know." Danny reached for Sammy's hand. "Let's go."

"On that note, Evan, let's go get the paint and I'll show you what we need." Evan followed him and never said a word.

* * * * * * *

Following, Ruthie considered her daddy warning the boys, 'I want those rabbits there when I return.' Surely two little boys wouldn't disregard daddy, would they? She had to keep her eye on them today. Any picture in her mind of the baby bunnies was pushed aside by seeing Evan in his blue shirt standing at a gravesite crying. Ruthie tried to pay attention. If she could spend time beneath the angel's spread wings she could meditate on what God was telling her. You are the messenger. The words sank into her consciousness. She could help others but she could not help herself. If God wanted to use her, why then was she seeing visions that seemed real of Evan just as she had seen a flash of Haley in the grip of an older man, a man she had seen at Haley's wedding? And now there was a new happening with Haley.

So deep were her thoughts, Ruthie waited until the boys were engrossed in building skyscrapers with their blocks, she returned to lock the door that led to the garden to prevent any planned escape and allowed herself to try to connect the double visions she was seeing. Surely there was no connection between Haley and Evan. She tried to shake off the inner workings of her mind. Her task for the day were not that difficult, watch the older twins, Danny and Sammy, and if they were good they could go into the garden and help her pull clover from the day lilies, but that changed with their idea for the bunnies. Going through the house she pressed the small lock the boys could not reach at the top of the door and went back to Holly and

Noel's playroom. Jewel had Noel sitting beside her in the big rocking chair and Holly on her lap as she read, "No, Sam I am." She glanced up to smile at Ruthie. "These two are already tired and about to go to sleep."

"I'll be in the music room," Ruthie said, "Near Danny and Sammy. I don't trust them today."

"Any reason why?" Jewel asked. "I saw Evan painting the front posts, is that the problem?"

"There're new baby rabbits in the flower garden. I hope they're not planning something." She heard Jewel chuckling as she went on down the hall and peeped into the boy's room. They were there.

Shortly Jewel joined her, baby monitor in her hand which she sit on the piano. "What are we doing in here?"

"Just putting the sheet music back where it belongs and dusting the furniture." A fresh vision of Evan flashed in her memory. "Jewel, does Evan talk about his family, specifically his Mom and Dad?"

"Evan hardly talks about anyone," Jewel replied. "Why? Is that important?" Ruthie took her by the hand and led her to the bay window. "Something's bothering you, Ruthie, I can tell. What is it?"

"What do you know about me that's unusual, Jewel?"

"You are easy to talk with, you are much older in your understanding than most your age." Jewel was thinking. "I don't know if I'm supposed to know but I think you sometime receive messages from God, about things that are going to happen. Is that right? No one mentions it, do they? Why?"

"No, they don't and yes, you are right. I don't know why God chose me to do this. My Momma and Bitty who was my sitter said it is a gift from God, they said much like discernment, whatever that means." Ruthie laughed. "Sometimes it makes me sad, but when someone's ill and I lay my hands on them and pray even if they don't know I'm praying and they get better, then I'm happy and glad I have this gift."

"You are worried about Evan?" Ruthie averted her gaze. "It's all right, Ruthie, I can tell when you seem to want to speak with him at times but you never do. I sense it but I'm pretty sure Evan has no idea."

"I need to talk to him, Jewel, but I don't know how to do this. I think, in time, if God wants me to, it will happen."

"Are we in danger, Ruthie?"

"No, not danger, but from what I feel inside whatever is going on with Evan can affect your future."

"Our marriage?" Jewel's countenance changed to sadness. "I want our lives to be happy, Ruthie, and different from what my parents have. They don't know how to laugh or be mischievous and yet they are content but I've seen your parents laugh and hug each other and us and they are so in love. I want that."

* * * * * *

The week was closing out. On Friday the day dawned beautiful and bright. Ruthie and Jewel had the house sparkling clean; all the clothes were laundered, folded and put away. Food was Daniel's department. "Does your daddy always plan the holiday gatherings?" Jewel asked, curious to this new arrangement, different from her family customs. He does, Ruthie had assured her. His family owns a hotel that often caters to social activities of the community and that part of the business was left to Daddy Daniel. "That's very unusual." Jewel remarked. "I like it. Is there anything else going to happen?"

"If its warm weather we have an egg hunt." She saw surprise in Jewel's eyes. "You are thinking an egg hunt is pagan, because we studied that in our church last week, but Momma and daddy adopted the new way. "We have eggs dressed in costume," she giggled. "Remember the weekend the mommas sold cookies? Well, after, donating the money they made to a community cause, they met to decorate and fill the eggs. The day of the egg hunt whoever finds the special eggs has to bring them to complete the story and they win a small prize. You'll see. It's a lot of fun and full of surprise."

"Can you explain? I don't understand."

"We all have eggs. Everyone brings them and everyone hunts them. We use plastic." Ruthie grinned. "The adults have as much fun as anyone."

"How do you dress an egg?" Jewel was truly perplexed. "You said costumes."

"I'll show you. Come with me." First, Ruthie peeped into the twins rooms and found them playing. "I just know Sammy is planning something," she explained. "He may forget for a while, but then he remembers." Jewel followed into the family room to the library wall of top shelves and bottom cabinets with doors. Ruthie pulled a picture album from behind a set of doors and laying it on a table found the pictures from previous years of eggs with painted costumes and head bands depicting Easter characters.

"Here are the disciples. See? The egg has a head scarf with a band and then a piece of cloth for a robe. There are twelve and one is dressed in black. That's Judas. Here's Jesus in the white robe, then the two thieves for the cross on each side of Jesus only have a wrap around their waist."

She glanced up to see understanding dawning in Jewel's face. "Oh, this must be Mary and the other two women who went to the tomb but who are all the extra eggs with only painted faces?"

"The extra eggs are all that gathered at the cross that day." Ruthie explained. "Marigold created the first set. She sent the design into a company that painted the egg costumes on them and she sells them in her shop." Ruthie returned the album to the cabinet. "When we finish the hunt we hear the story and say an Easter prayer."

Jewel was taking time to absorb the information. She and Ruthie stared at each other, Ruthie waiting for Jewel's thought on the matter and Jewel comparing what she heard to her own experience. Finally she said, "I guess it's all right. I've never hunted Easter eggs as I was taught it's pagan to do so."

"Let Momma explain it to you. She said before Christianity took hold in our world to some countries Easter was a celebration of Spring. After that, she will have to tell you because there's a lot to the story."

"Well," Jewel seemed resigned to the information, "At least your friends children will remember the true story from the Bible and not that a rabbit is responsible. It's important we know Jesus died on the cross for our sins, isn't it?" She tied the strings to her apron and picked up the dusting cloth. "Do you think we need to check on the boys since Holly and Noel are still sleeping?"

* * * * * *

Anne was frustrated. "I don't know what to do Little Momma." Olivia stopped folding the children's clothes and turned to Anne. "Andrew said we've been served additional papers. Now the judge has us in contempt of court for my leaving with the children but you and I know they were coming for them after Andrew had words with the Judge."

"What are you thinking?" Little Momma riffled her fingers through her spiked hair on top and smoothed it at the base of her neck. She was wearing knee shorts that revealed her beautifully tanned skin. The children were still sleeping and she and Anne were preparing for another day on the beach after feeding Andy and Addy.

"If we go home, they are sure to come for Adeline." Anne's eyes clouded with tears. "How can I let that happen? She has lost her mother and now according to Andrew's anonymous caller, it isn't Mrs. Walden wants her; she wants to give Adeline to some stranger who can't have a baby." The tears ran down her cheek. "Why can't that person adopt a child?"

"Perhaps her history of life not good." Little Momma sank onto the nearest chair. "I know of such, when the court appoints someone to check history, then all will be revealed and when revealed not so good."

"Should we go home, Little Momma, or take our chances and stay?"

"Whatever you decide, I help you." She sighed, heavily burdened for Anne. "You wrong about one thing; Adeline's mother did not die. Her real mother gave her to you and you did not die. You are mother."

A sob caught in Anne's throat. "I feel like she's mine. I would never have been able to accept this had not Ellen stayed with me, always listening and caring enough about me to explain the plan of salvation to me that I might be saved." She dabbed at her eyes with the bottom of her shirt. "MY life changed. I found courage to stand up to Andrew." She smiled. "Yes, Little Momma, he was a bad boy in those days. Otherwise we wouldn't have Adeline, would we?"

"That still no way to treat a wife."

"I certainly agree on that. Now," Anne's shoulders drooped. "We have to pray and decide, stay or go."

Andrew called that night. "Oh," disappointment was in his voice. "You're still there? I had hoped you were on your way home. Anne, I can't convince the Judge we should have Addy, she's mine and yours."

"She is ours, Andrew." Andrew heard those words and little else as he hung up. She wasn't coming home but he loved her. Anne had turned into a force and right now that's what he needed. Strength.

CHAPTER 11

"Look at our crew. Ruthie come on out here." There had never been a happier prouder daddy. Daniel was waiting for Ruthie and Holly to come down the hall. Ruthie was dressed early. When she volunteered to dress Holly, Daniel and Ellen were busy dressing Sammy and Danny. "What do you mean Sammy refused to wear short pants?" He had questioned, forgetting the twins had grown out of the toddler stage. "So," he said, "Noel wears the short pants and knee socks and the big boys are wearing long pants."

"You got it, Daddy of the year," Ellen replied, finishing with Noel. "Now, go line them up and get a picture if you can. Ruthie is ready and has dressed Holly. You're going to be a proud daddy."

For five minutes maybe she would have the room to herself and she wanted to pick up the straggle of sleeping garments since their friends would be arriving by one o'clock. The dinner was in the warming oven, Daniel had the tables set up and Jewel and Ruthie had the house in mint condition. Working the week, she was ever thankful for the two who kept the twins and the house clean. For a moment her mind flashed to the two women she suspected were still sleeping in the extra room at the clinic. Their house keeping of the rooms and office were immaculate, therefore Dr. Lonzo had no complaint. For a second she wondered what food they would be eating today, but they were not Christian and did not observe Easter.

Easter had its beautiful sincere meaning. She prayed she and Daniel were doing their best with the children understanding the reason for the day of celebration. "No, it isn't Jesus birthday," she explained to Sammy on Saturday. "It is the day Jesus rose from the grave after dying for our sins."

"Do I sin, Mommy?" His little face was serious, his eyes troubled, Ellen had to hug him to reassure him he often did things that weren't what he should but she didn't believe he was sinning yet, since he was just out of the toddler stage. "I don't ever want to hurt you Mommy." She received the best kiss. Still, before leaving the room and her comforting arms, he had to ask, "Does Danny sin, Mommy?"

"Not yet, Sweetheart. Sin is when you have a choice; you think about it and know its wrong but do it anyway."

"Then we sin." Tears ran down his cheeks. "Me and Danny both sinned 'cause we thought about what we did and Daddy said not to but we did it anyway." He burst into uncontrollable sobbing which brought Danny running to his side and soon the two were howling together with Daniel coming to ask why.

* * * * * *

"Boys," Daniel gave them his best daddy look. "Are you ready to sit still and listen to the Easter reading as Brother Joe and the choir present it?" Danny and Sammy stared at their mother first afraid she would tell daddy what they had done. She only smiled and reassured them everything was all right. "If you are quiet you can sit with us, but if you aren't we will have to take you back to Miss Mary. The choir has put a lot of work into today's service, so we must appreciate them."

The twins stared at each other and then said together, "We'll be good, Daddy." Daniel smiled and opened his hand, "one on each side," he said and they gripped his fingers. Ellen winked at Ruthie, as Ruthie settled Holly on her hip and Ellen carried Noel.

"We are quite an eyeful, aren't we, Sweetums?" Ruthie grinned. "Does it hurt you carrying Holly, seems like you have to keep her on your hip or you would lose her. I'll take her if it hurts you or if you want."

"I'm used to carrying her like this, Momma. I do it all the time. You know that."

Ellen laughed. They were near the entrance. "Yes, I know, but at home in short distance is different. Oh, there's Jewel and Evan. Don't they look handsome?"

"I told Jewel she was really pretty and it embarrassed her."

"Well, my darling Sweetums, you are beautiful. Here we are. Now we can let them down and hold their hand or they'll get away from us. These two are going to Nursery. I know they wouldn't be quiet."

Pastor Joe greeted them. "We miss you two in choir this year. Don't do that to us next year. You hear?"

"There was no way we could this year with these twins," Dan replied. "Maybe three from now."

"Is that kids or years?" Daniel squeezed Pastor Joe's shoulder. "Years, brother. Years." They laughed.

* * * * * * *

The lights began to lower until everyone was settled in their seat. Ellen silently took count to see that all invited for dinner were attending. Harriet sit with Marigold and Matt's family and by her side was Andrew. She knew Andrew well enough to know he was sad and missing Anne and the kids. The Gipson's were across the aisle and Haley and Jeremy were with them. Jewel and Evan sit behind the group. Ellen smiled, they were holding hands and that was the first typical action of a dating couple she had seen between them. Just as the choir filed in and everyone was being seated, Daniel gave her a nudge in the ribs. Dr. Lonzo was walking down the aisle and it appeared everyone knew him. As he advanced each row of pews someone stood to shake his hand and welcome him. Dr. Lonzo merely smiled and continued to the pew where Ellen and Dan were. Everyone scooted and he slid in by Ruthie.

Leaning across Ruthie, Ellen whispered. "I'm honored to see you here, Doctor." His smile widened.

"Let us rise for the first hymn on this day honoring our Savior who died for us."

The scenes began to unfold; Jesus carried the cross until Simon of Cyrene was told to help him. Then it was the scene on the cross and Jesus mother's sadness brought Sammy and Danny into Ellen's arms. Tears ran down their face as Ellen tucked one on each side of her body and kissed their forehead. Ruthie took Danny's hand while Daniel held Sammy's. Jewel had become protective of the twins and Ellen wondered if their tears made her want to comfort them but when she glanced to where Jewel and Evan were sitting the two had left. She tried to dismiss their absence saying everything was all right but she was concerned. She looked to Ruthie, perhaps she had an idea.

Pastor Joe read the scripture; "When he had cried with a loud voice Jesus yielded up his spirit. And behold, the vail of the temple was rent in twain from the top to the bottom and the earth did quake and the rocks rent. And the graves were opened and many bodies of the saints which slept, rose and came out of the graves after His resurrection and went into the Holy city and appeared to many. And when the evening come there was a rich man of Arimathae, named Joseph, who also was Jesus disciple. He went to Pilate and begged the body of Jesus and Pilate commanded the body to be delivered. And when Joseph had taken the body, he wrapped it in a clean linen cloth and laid it in his own new tomb which he had hewn out of rock and he rolled a great stone at the door of the sepulcher and departed."

Ruthie ignored her mother. I'm only seven years old her countenance seemed to say. I don't know any thing. There was clapping. That made Ellen's attention return to the scene where Jesus arose from the grave. The twins must approve for they were happily clapping their hands. Two angels stood by the tomb. Pastor Joe read the scripture about the women going to cleanse Jesus body. The angels turned to face the audience. Ellen's heart quickened as her mind went into overdrive. It was Evan and Jewell. They sang like angels. She wondered when Jewel practiced. Now Ruthie was smiling. Ellen was sure she knew. She reached around Danny and hugged Ruthie, "You little scamp, you've been holding out on me."

"The Sabbath ended," Pastor Joe read, "as it began to dawn toward the first day of the week and Mary Magdalene and the other Mary came to the Sepulcher. Behold there was a great earthquake and the Angel of the Lord descended from Heaven and came and rolled back the stone from the door and sat upon it. The Angel said to the women, Fear ye not, for I know that ye seek Jesus which was crucified. He is not here for he is risen as he said, come, see the place where they laid the Lord. Go quickly now and tell his disciples he is risen from the dead and behold he goeth before you into Galilee; there shall ye see him; lo I have told you."

Jewel stepped forward, for the second song, her arms outstretched, the light from above beaming down on Jewel's face and making the feathered wings glisten. Everyone was enraptured of Jewel's singing and then Evan joined her. Remarkable, Ellen thought, rejoicing that the church had allowed Jewel and Evan the spotlight of the presentation and how well they performed. Surely the two had missed their calling.

* * * * * *

"It looks like a parade." Ruthie's voice was happy as she clapped her hands and the twins joined in.

"I hope no one thinks we are headed to a cemetery," Dan said through pressed lips to Ellen.

"Why would they think that?" She gave him a puzzled glance, and then, staring down the road saw traffic pull to one side to let them pass. "What is going on? There's no h-e-a-r-s-e."

"No, just a black S-U-V," he spelled, shaking his head. "You can bet Harper is laughing his head off."

"Well, look on the bright side, Daddy of the Year, we will arrive quicker this way, all of us at once."

"So much for having a few things accomplished before the guest arrive, huh?"

"H-o-r-s-e." Is that what you spelled, Momma? I think you made a mistake."

"So what are you looking forward to, Ruthie?"

"The egg hunt, Jewel has never been allowed to hunt eggs. I told her Marigold invented a new Easter hunt." Ruthie scanned the sky. "It's not going to rain is it, Daddy?"

Cars were double parked to where the new house property began and around the corner of their own. "All right, guys, listen up." Marigold took charge. "You know how it is when you have guests. You need a few minutes to keep down chaos. Let's line the little ones up for pictures and give them about thirty minutes since we arrived together. First, we'll get Harper and Dorothy's picture and then Harriet's, so they can go in and help Ellen. Ready Gipson's?"

Everyone was happy on a beautiful warm day to follow Marigold's instructions as she led them into Ellen's garden and posed them against the various features, and to sit when their time was over in the wonderful swings and garden chairs visiting and exploring the new plants Daniel had started for the new year. Matt had both children settled firmly on his lap watching as Marigold did her magic. Then it was his and Marigold's time and Andrew took the camera. He had just finished when the group from Newhaven arrived, Stephen Silvi leading the way, his new bride from Christmas waving excitedly to the garden crew. There was much hugging and laughter as they all come together and then the Merkel's arrived with the new baby. Ruthie waited to watch the twins when everyone rushed to see him.

Levi and Leah allowed everyone to examine their off-spring but all the while Leah was searching the group for Ruthie. It was Marigold noticed and sent Andrew to watch the twins along with Matt who was already in the garden. "Tell Ruthie to come see the baby. Leah is waiting for her."

Ruthie came running as Leah handed the baby to Levi and opened her arms. "Where were you?" she asked, hugging Ruthie to her chest. "Oh, Ruthie, I can't wait for you to know our little boy."

"How is little Jim, I mean, how is Jeremiah?" Leah gave her a startled look and then settled onto one of the concrete benches along the path to the garden. Ruthie laughed. "I know about your not being able to decide his name right now."

"Actually, we did call him Jim but it just didn't feel right and when we called him Jeremiah, he was a different baby as if he knew and understood." She sighed, heavily. "We could have used you there as our soundboard."

"Does he like Jeremiah Isaiah?"

"Ruthie." Leah stooped down to hug Ruthie to her side. "How do you know these things?"

"Just remember what Momma told you the day we were at your house after the shooting in the park."

"Who got shot in the park?" Marigold caught up with them as they turned toward the house. "By the way Ellen says everything is ready. But what about who got shot in the park?"

"No, one, Silly." Ruthie caught hold of Marigold's swinging hand. "You know the story."

Quite dramatically, Marigold replied, "Yes, but we've a million memories and a few dozen new stories since then. So let's go eat and see if that curbs our desire to talk about the past." To Leah, she said, "I'm so happy you and Levi were able to come today."

"We couldn't let this pass us by, not with Mabel and Nate and the Silvi's coming." Leah chuckled, "Would you believe the Silvi's are still in the honeymoon stage. We see them often because they are Jeremiah's God parents."

"What's a God parent?" Ruthie stopped in the path to hear the answer.

"Some parents ask a dear friend to step in and watch over their children, that's if anything should happen to the real parents, then someone will see to their needs."

"Like Anne and Andrew took in Addy?" Ruthie asked because she was worried about Annie leaving. "Sometimes I see Anne in my mind and she is sad and there's a policeman with her, but not Addy."

"Is it a dream, Ruthie?"

"No, Marigold, it's what I see in my mind, not when I'm asleep but I'm awake, like a while ago."

"That doesn't sound good, but whatever God shows you is always for the glory of God and to help someone in our midst." Marigold gave Ruthie an understanding smile and said, "I think if we don't hurry in, your mom's going to make mincemeat of us." She paused a minute, thinking. "Did either of you see Britany or Pookie in the group? I'm just curious."

"No, it was better they didn't come." Ruthie was astonished as Marigold. "I don't know why I said that." Already Ruthie was looking within and what she saw was not good. "Momma said I must not speak in haste. I must always consider what God gives me before sharing it, because I am young."

Everyone was in high spirits. Daniel said grace and explained about the seating arrangement. "We have the children's table in the corner to give them plenty room but after that you choose where you want to sit. So now…it's time to dig in."

Ruthie sat beside Leah and Levi. "What's new, Ruthie?" Levi was enjoying seeing all the new friends he and Leah had made due to the Revival at Newhaven's Shining Light Church. "We've not had any more fires," he confessed, "because of a faulty piece of equipment, nor shooting's in town. About all we've done is produce a son that we couldn't decide on a name for him. Now, what do you think of that?"

"I knew that and I thought it was funny." Ruthie giggled. "I guess Michael still likes to play cards?"

"Aw, yes." Levi made a face, reminiscent of Michael when he was on to something big in the game he loved. "Michael is a whiz, according to Leah, at math and since it's difficult for some he hides his ability to work the problems easily. Isn't that what you said, Hon?"

"Yes, he's embarrassed but he still likes you, Ruthie. I see your name on his binder."

"That's nice," Ruthie replied, but I'll probably not see Michael again for a long time, years even." She saw Ellen getting ready to make a plate and excused herself, "I need to see my Momma."

She caught up with Ellen as she searched for another set of silverware. "Momma, I keep seeing Anne and she is in trouble, I think. She is on the phone while someone is saying, "but the child is not yours." Are they talking about Addy? It worries me, Momma. Anne looks really worried."

"Let me think on this as we eat. I really wish we could have helped Anne here at home but there was nothing we could do."

"But Momma, what do they mean the child is not yours. Addy is theirs because her mother gave her to them."

"Sometimes the law has a say in who raises a child." Ellen saw the concern in Ruthie's eyes. "Sweetums, don't worry, just let me speak with Andrew."

The laughter was a continuous happy sound as everyone visited and caught up on what was happening in family lives when suddenly a lull began by the door, someone had come in and they were not part of the invited group from Newhaven or the church. All eyes were on a dark haired woman and two men in suits.

Without any courtesy at all, she took the glass from Mabel, a fork from Nate and pecked on the glass. Everyone came to attention. "I am here for the child, Adeline, Summer Walton's daughter." No one spoke a word. "These two gentlemen are from the Federal Bureau of Investigation, if you withhold evidence that Adeline is on this property you are in danger of spending the next five to ten years in a prison cell." No one spoke. "Go through each room, destroy it if you must as you search for Adeline."

"One minute." Daniel stepped forward. "This is a private home; do you have a search warrant?"

She smirked. "These, sir, are FBI agents, in case you haven't heard they do as they think best in insinuating circumstances to come to the truth of the matter and we have learned the gathering here today constitutes friends of Andrew and Anne Graves. Now, move aside and we shall continue the business that brought us to your home today. We do not need a search warrant."

Every man present lined up behind Daniel, their eyes on the two agents and no one blinked. The agents first thought to bluff but they were outnumbered. "It would be a Federal Offense to strike an agent."

"Lady," Harper Gipson stepped to the front. "There are three of you. Have you counted our number?" Stocky and built like a bull, Harper made a good front for the others. "Now, lady, you need to take your thugs, which I very much doubt are FBI, and tuck your tail between your legs and hurry on down the road."

"That wasn't nice, Harper," Dorothy whispered.

"No? But it was appropriate."

"Never a dull moment around here," Daniel quipped as they heard a car drive away."We are prone to say what's next?" Everyone was laughing when the door opened. Dr.Lonzo let out a yelp and hurried to embrace Little Momma. Next, Anne carrying Adeline

Grace came through, her eyes on Andrew as he stopped mid-sentence telling Evan he wished the previous visitors had been his wife and children. Just at that moment, Andy peeped around his Mother's skirt, saw his daddy and started running to him.

Ruthie caught her mother's eye and smiled. Ellen opened her arms and Ruthie walked into them for a hug. "Well Sweetums, we didn't have to worry long over that, did we?" But Ruthie dropped her head. "You don't think it's over?" Ellen closed her eyes for a moment, thinking and finally said, "No, it isn't."

"This is quite a reunion, Anne." Daniel was elated. "I've worried over our boy here." He laid an arm around Andrew's shoulders. "I think he's missed you more than any of us can imagine."

"It's mutual," Anne was saying her hand in Andrew's. "I've come back because he ask me to, otherwise we would have stayed to keep Addy safe but Andrew feels the judge would order Andy be put in one of the state homes or to a private sector. He's ours, why would they do that, Daniel?"

Daniel was shaking his head, "I don't know, Anne. It's all strange to me. Andrew is the lawyer. Ask him."

"It makes no sense." Daniel began as the doorbell rang and Ellen answered. He saw the two policemen and wondered that they arrived so quickly. "They must have left something and sent these officers," he looked around. "I don't see anything."

One officer produced a paper. "Are you Andrew Graves?"

Andrew stepped forward, "That would be me."

"Is Anne Graves present?"

Anne was returning from changing Adeline's clothes when she heard the questions. Evan was coming down the hall from the opposite direction. Anne put a finger to her lips and motioned for silence. "Take Adeline and go out into the garden and sit on the bench beneath the angel's wings and do not come out until you know for sure the police officers have left. Ellen always keeps a shawl or light blanket hanging by the back door. Take it for Adeline." She kissed Adeline and then hugged Evan. "Thank you."

"If you withhold evidence that Mrs. Graves is present…."

Anne stepped from the hallway into view, smiling though her heart was breaking. "Did someone call my name?"

"Andrew Graves. Anne Graves." The first officer spoke their names, his head bowed, while the second officer looked on. "Mr. Andrew Graves. Mrs. Anne Graves, you are under arrest for contempt of court. You will be housed in the County Jail until either a called meeting of the court or until regular court day. We have orders to take you there. Now."

Harriet stepped forward. "Officer, I seem to recall you from several years back when our friend's little girl was kidnapped. Now, do you have to take these two friends of mine in this afternoon, or is there the slightest chance you have not actually located them and by their own cognizance they will turn their selves in tomorrow in order to work more closely with the court and the Judge who ordered their arrest?" She turned to Andrew. "I believe any court works better with one who turns themselves in, is that correct, Andrew?"

"That is correct."

"I believe Officer, you were in trouble for not sounding an Amber Alert early on during the kidnapping of my friend's little daughter and I, since I knew the captain, ask lenience for you, so it would be only fair if you looked the other way this one time to return the courtesy I extended to you."

The second officer stepped forward to protest, "That…"

"That is the best thing you can think of, also, Officer Bailey? Yes, I know your name. I was on the council that heard about the last little escapade you were involved in. Perhaps you saw where Harriet Becker came to your defense and ask that your peers give you another chance? I serve on several community boards." She spoke to Ellen's guests as she said, "Officer Bailey had a little fender bender in the Police Car he was driving but we really don't have to know why."

"But that's black mail," Officer Bailey sputtered.

"Oh, no, Officer, it is job security." She turned, searching for Ellen. "Ellen, don't you think the officers would love a plate and finish it off with that delicious Crème la Apple pie Dorothy brought? It will give us an opportunity to know who serves on our Police force and we will all be better informed when things pertaining to the community happen."

"Now that is a brib….."

"Stop, while we are ahead, Bailey," the first officer snapped. "You want to be the one sitting in jail?" The two turned to take the plates Ellen and Anne had loaded for them. Perspiration had darkened the back of their uniforms but no one made mention.

Ruthie watched in amazement as the officers were treated as best friends to the group, but Jewel was astonished. "Does this family make friends of everyone?" She asked. "Next they will be praying."

Bailey, the officer was looking around for the baby. As far as he could tell there were four babies and none resembled the picture that young black headed lady ask them to study. "Are you sure we are at the right place?" He asked his partner. "There's not a little girl here matches the description."

CHAPTER 12

Officer Hankens waited for Daniel to finish his story. "Sir," he said, "we are leaving. Thank you for the good food." He hesitated to finish, knowing Daniel understood there was something he needed to say. "Sir, can I trust Mr. and Mrs. Graves to come in tomorrow?" His countenance seemed to fall, momentarily, "If they don't, Sir, it will be my and Bailey's job." He dropped his head nearly to his chest.

"I can promise you that without a second thought," Daniel replied. "You may recall, Mr. Graves is an attorney. His word is his livelihood." Reaching out to shake the officer's hand he added, "It would be God's blessing if you gave them until around one, to get their son settled with Mrs. Becker." Daniel noticed Officer Bailey was waiting outside. "We would like to pray safety for you and officer Bailey." Hankens motioned Bailey back inside as he followed Daniel to where the guest sit in a circle around the room. "I'm going to ask the two of you to stand in the midst of us, that we may direct the prayer upon you." Daniel pinned his eyes upon Harper. "Come lead us, brother," he said and Harper stepped forward.

"Lord God, we come asking forgiveness for our sins but we come with hearts filled with joy and thankfulness that you, Lord, the King of Glory saw our need and when we ask, you came into our hearts to live within us, comforting us when we are sad, rejoicing with us during times of joy. You are our Father and we thank you. We have had such misery connected to problems in the last two years, but you know what goes on inside of us. You are the great physician, you heal our heart, our mind and allow us mercy that we might go on and walk this path because of your great love. Now Lord, in a time when our people who serve under the badge of Police work need you, we come asking that you bless the officers as they stand before you. Officers Bailey and Hankins need your protection as they go into places that have problems. We ask you to be with them daily, watch over them in those moments of danger, Lord, keep them safe is our prayer and we thank you that we can talk with you. We love you and we praise you and we ask in your name. Amen.

Finished praying, Harper put out a hand and the officers shook his hand and the other men's. "We will keep you both in our prayers for safety," Daniel said, in parting. Once they had backed out the drive and headed toward the city, Daniel blew out a breath of hot air and fixed his eyes on Andrew. "Come forward, brother, come on Anne" he said and to those in the circle he motioned they gather around and lay a hand on Andrew and Anne. "Let us pray God keeps his hand of protection on our friends, that no matter the length of time required to find closure they will feel his presence. Ellen, will you lead?"

"Jesus." Ellen paused, letting the name of God's son sink into their mind. "Heavenly Father, we just want to praise you." Again, as one, they listened and allowed their hearts to be in tune. "We praise you Lord, that Anne and the children and Little Momma have returned to us, safe. Lord, we do not know the plans you are making for their future but we trust in you, that their lives will be together as was Summer's plan when she stated Andrew is Adeline's father and it was her desire that Anne become Adeline's mother. Lord, we trust in you that the hands of those who would separate them for selfish reasons will be tied. We are united in friendship that you have given to us, and we thank you for that bond we share and that you hear our prayer for Anne and Andrew. We have placed this in your hands as we have lift their names to you. We praise you Heavenly Father and we thank you for your son who died on the cross for our sins that we might have eternal life. We love you. We pray in your name. Amen.

"Perfect ending for a perfect day," Harper boomed. "Now let's go home, Dorothy. Where's our daughter? There you are Haley. Jeremy, let's see if we are parked where we can go on home."

Haley whispered to Marigold, "That's my dad, the biggest voice in the neighborhood but a heart to match. God bless Harper Gipson."

"Amen." Marigold replied, hooking an arm around Haley's shoulders, she whispered. "Have you told Jeremy, yet?" Haley dropped her head. "I take that's a no, hmmm." Marigold shook her head.

They were near the door, where the Merkals were collecting baby paraphernalia when Leah glanced up and said, "here, Haley, hold Jimmy. I declare we have enough stuff to capsize a boat. How is it, when it unravels, so to speak it appears twice as much as when you bring it? If it's all right with you, I'll run these items to the car and then relieve you of my baby."

"Let's set over here," Marigold offered, her hand on Haley's arm leading the way. Away from the others, Haley examined the chubby little boy. He yawned, opened his eyes and smiled at her.

"Oh," she stared hard to see if he smiled again. He did. "Marigold, he's precious." She fit him closer to her body. "Oh, Marigold, how could anyone abort a baby?" She placed her hand where he would close his own around her fingers. "Ooooh," she was captured. He smiled at the sound of her voice as his fingers tightened. Tears formed in her eyes ready to spill over. "God gave me this moment, didn't he?" Her voice though hushed was filled with the wonder only a new baby can bring. She closed her eyes. "Thank you, Jesus," she said as Marigold's hold tightened on her shoulder. "Thank you, Jesus."

Marigold felt the wonder of the moment. Closing her eyes she remembered the birth of her own. "It's something a mother cannot explain," she whispered. "I came wondering about time I needed to do laundry this afternoon, but I'm going home with a blessing no amount of laundering could have given."

Leah joined them. She felt a change had been wrought and though she had no idea of the content of that change, the feeling in her heart knew it was good. Whatever had happened, she need not ask, the feeling multiplied as she took her baby boy and leaned to kiss Haley and then Marigold on the cheek. "We are so blessed," she said. "Our marriage was becoming stale and God gave us a son. Praise his holy name. What we could not do for ourselves, he did for us. I pray for others in need as we were."

Jewel and Evan were coming in from the garden. Adeline was wrapped loosely in the blanket, one foot dangling out and her eyes fixed on Evan. He lift her up onto his shoulder and she reached for his hair, a smile of contentment on her face as it coiled around her fingers.

"I think she likes you," Marigold said, rising up, "Look at those little fat cheeks. How are you little Adeline?" Adeline responded by laying her head on Evan's shoulder, pressing closer as she smiled. "What now?" an expression of concern surfaced, "Who will keep the children while Anne and Andrew check in at the court house?" Marigold's question was mirrored in the faces of the other's. "Not family services. Who?" She glanced quickly to where Andrew and Anne were in discussion with the Gates.

"We would love to." Evan and Jewel replied together. "Is it possible, do you think?"

"Not unless you are married," Marigold replied. "Anne learned a bit about that. Just google and you'll find out."

The two fastened their eyes on each other. "Why not?" Evan asked. "That would just set the date up a week or so. We could do something for Anne and Andrew for a change." He was smiling. "Would that be all right with you, Jewel?"

She nodded. "It may not please my parents but the reason is worthy. Yes."

The words were barely out of her mouth when the door burst open. The black haired lady was with two different officers. "We will have either the parents in jail or the child with Family Services. Which is it?" The two with her did not so much as bat an eye. Andrew and Anne had heard and were coming toward them.

"Take care of our babies," Anne whispered, as tears streamed down her cheeks. "I thought this was settled for us to come in tomorrow, noon."

"I waited to hear the outcome," the black haired lady replied. "So what did you do, bribe the previous officers? We knew you had to be picked up; otherwise you would skip out on us. Cuff them."

Andrew and Anne were led from the room handcuffed by the officers; the black haired lady was smiling. "It does not pay to mess with the law."

"No, it doesn't," Daniel replied, holding the Bible high. "God is still in charge, Mrs. Black. Wait and see." They were all speechless, thinking it had been settled to see it reopened so soon. "Take your responsibility fully tonight, and let us pray over this situation that God's hand of mercy doesn't allow these children in a foster home, but instead the law allow them to stay with Harriet or the Gates as offered." Mrs. Black didn't bother to answer. She slipped out the door behind the officers with Andrew and Anne. Those inside heard the doors to the Police car shut as the motor revved ready to leave the premises and a second car driven by the woman followed.

"I was completely shocked silent," Marigold quoted. "Just when I thought they were going to get a break." Shaking her head, she asked, "Daniel, who is that woman you called Mrs. Black?"

"I made a call. As I understand, the Judge has already chosen her as a friend of the court. That is highly unusual which Andrew and I discussed; the lady wanting Addie must have a lot of pull."

"Or a lot of wealth," Marigold muttered. "She, Mrs. Black, seems to think it is already cut and dried that whoever the party is she represents will have Adeline when this matter comes to a close."

"That being the case, it will never close. Andrew and Anne will fight for Adeline."

* * * * * * *

Running on adrenalin, Ellen and Daniel were able to put the children to bed and with Evan and Jewel's help put the house back in order. "This is no small feat, having twenty six people in for an evening luncheon after church service," Daniel mused, aloud. "Are you all right, Ellen?"

"It was enjoyable until the Police came for Andrew and Anne. Leaving their children was horrible for them." Daniel paused from cleaning around the children's table, waiting for the answer to his question. "Yes," she replied, "I'm fine. Everyone helped with the food storage; it is always good to be together." She sighed. "I can't help but worry over them, leaving their babies with us…"

"Jewel and I would like to be married in order to help with the children," Evan said. "Would that upset you terribly? We could keep them in their own home. Do you think their parents' would let us?"

Ellen sit down, at the table, surprised Evan and Jewel were considering such a responsibility and whether the judge would go for it. "What do you think, Daniel?"

"We have no leverage."

"What do you mean?"

"Again, this is what Andrew and I were discussing. It is a trumped up charge against them; someone is making waves and when it is a fake charge pushed through, sad to say, Andrew said if you don't have something of equal seriousness against the one making charges or the judge who allows it, you have very little chance of winning. In this case we are speaking of bond being denied, no doubt, and even tomorrow they will do their best to add more charges to keep them away from the children and in that regard it's going to get ugly."

"Which means the parents may be in jail for a length of time based on contempt of court, not following the decree of the papers that were served."

"But Anne left before Andrew was served."

"Yes," Daniel replied, patiently, "But who was served papers first?" He nodded. "Anne. And she left."

Ellen considered the truth of his statement. "I pray the children feel safe with us, we've not kept them before." She saw Evan fidgeting; this man who rarely said two words had something to say. "What are you thinking, Evan?"

"If there was the slightest chance a Judge would leave the children in our care, would you feel it inconsiderate of us if we moved our wedding date closer in order to take care of Andrew and Anne's children, that is, if they aren't allowed to come home?"

"I saw how Addy clung to you, Evan, and it's obvious Andy feels comfortable with both of you." She sighed, "Are you sure it's what you want? It would be answered prayer for the children."

"Let's not get ahead of ourselves," Daniel cautioned. "First, we need to see if they can be released on bail. If that happens, meaning until their court date, then the next step is to sign papers saying they have given permission for Jewel and Evan, but first steps first, meaning they have to prove to the judge they want complete custody of Adeline, and on what grounds and that would possibly be Andrew proving he is the birth father and then Anne would need to bring the couple who stayed with Summer before the judge to prove Summer wanted them to raise Adeline. That would be before they even consider Evan and Jewel. Andrew was very explicit about the process this type of court case involves."

Ellen felt the throes of her friend's woes upon her own shoulders. Glancing one to the other, she did feel more comforted that they were not taking a quick way out, because that would surely fail, instead they were considering the whole picture. For a moment, she felt overwhelmed. It came to her; Jewel had sat quietly through their discussion. "Jewel?" She felt the need to hear from Jewel. "Jewel, please tell us your thoughts on this."

"I would be so honored to care for the children in the absence of their parents," she replied. "I'm certain the couple who kept Adeline would testify to the judge about her desire for the birth father and his wife to take custody of Addie but with the understanding of what has happened now we would step in for them but upon their release the children are returned to Anne and Andrew."

"You two are amazing and selfless that you would do that for a friend. What a role model you have become."

"If that were true," Jewel said softly, "We've had the best teachers; you and Mr. Daniel."

* * * * * *

Harriet eyed the clock, suspiciously aware some master mind had slowed the hands to an unheard of pace and the hour was slipping away, completely out of her grasp to help friends who had become like family. Her two companions for the morning would arrive shortly to take her to the Judges chamber. In her hand she held the paper that would make all the difference in Anne and Andrew's future days of being separated from their children. Could she pull this one off? The information was correct, she and her husband had lived through the situation but whether the Judge thought the information would hurt him or not was the question.

He was only thirty, starting his own practice when the situation occurred and her husband believing in him had worked the magic of thousands of dollars at his own expense in order to necessitate the Judge's credibility, for he was at that time a young attorney beginning his career. If there were times of payback that came her husband's way through the years she was unaware, but the piece of paper in her hand would either secure Anne and Andrew's getting out on bail or bring embarrassment to the Judge. The only power she had was to allow the information into public scrutiny and with the Judge ready to advance, to the last step of his career, before he retired he might not want the publicity it would bring.

* * * * * *

They arrived, escorting her to the black long line limo. "You always make me feel like queen for a day," she reminded them. "Thank you for all the years of service you have given me."

"You are completely welcome, Mrs. Becker and deserving of any attention we might add to your life."

Harriet chuckled, softly. "I don't know what to think of this one, boys. If the Judge is in a mood, then I have to counter him with just enough insinuation I'm open to taking him at his very worst and I intend to come out on the winning side." She paused. "Your job is to pull yourself up to your tallest height, stand by the door, one on each side as though you are not moving until I'm finished."

"We can handle that," the one who spoke before was nodding his head. "Yes, we can."

* * * * * *

"Harriet." The Judge acknowledged her. "You don't waste your time visiting, so tell me, what brings you down town?"

"I'm here on behalf of Anne and Andrew Graves and their unjust treatment at the hands of your men from our Police force, last night."

The Judge's eyes narrowed. "What is it you want, Harriet?"

"Release them on their own cognizance. Let the court prove Andrew's paternity and keep the children out of the system." She held a firm stare on the Judge. "As for Anne, there's nothing negative about her."

"I'm afraid I can't do that, Harriet." The Judge's smile only did lip service, his eyes were cold. "I'm afraid we have to abide according to the precepts of this type case. It is out of my hands. Your friends only have themselves to blame. The papers have already been recorded. I can't change that."

Harriet pulled the copy of the paper from her purse and laid it before the Judge. "Really?"

He read the first paragraph. A shudder went through his body, worse still he remembered exactly the situation as it had occurred and Mr. Becker's willingness to help him. When the old man died he had sighed with relief and now here stood Becker's wife before him. The information could ruin him.

"What did you say you wanted, Harriet?"

Harriet allowed a small smile to cross her lips. "Do your best," she replied as her escort stepped forward.

In the event he changed his mind, the two took a moment to step one on each side of the Judge. Harriet thought she saw a glimmer of sweat break out on his upper lip, "That's good," she said, to herself.

They delivered her in style back to her home. Harriet had to smile at the handsomeness of her escorts. They did her proud; young enough to be her sons, old enough to know good council when they saw it. She was often amazed the good fortune the Lord sent her way, marrying Mr. Becker when her heart was broken. His expectations were that she look good by his side and she had but she was always lonely.

She could only wonder was it loneliness that had made the man who now wore the robe and executed strict judgement on lesser men, by his own standards he was one of those, once. His moral and sinful downfall had been at the hands of a beautiful and notorious young woman, known for such escapades she had drawn him into her web and refused to let go when he realized he would not only lose his moral respectful family that he had brought to fruition himself, he would lose the career he had designed and offered to the public at large, who thought he was God's gift to those not born with a silver spoon in their mouth. How was it that men and women began with the best of interest for others and ended up thirty years later as contaminated as their worst clients?

Missing Andy and Addie, Harriet wandered the play room, picking up stray toys to place on the shelves. The Rainbow Palace had all of its figures in place and she studied the pattern. A momma, a daddy and brother, Andy was teaching Addy to say the names as they placed the tiny little pieces where they belonged, "We need a little girl like Addy," he said more than once. They must find a girl figurine.

"Lonesome, are you, Miz Harriet?" Hattie came from the kitchen carrying a dust pan and a broom. It was a time of caring. Miz Harriet didn't share a lot about what was happening to others in the group. Harriet handed over several pictures left by the others. "Aren't these pictures just precious? Our little girl look like a Princess and little Mr. Andy, he must be the Prince Brother or Brother Prince." Hattie laughed in her deep south voice. "I declare they do bring us such joy and satisfaction, don't they?"

"I don't know, Hattie, if you are aware someone is contesting Anne and Andrew's right to Adeline."

"Why, Miz Harriet. She done Mr. Andrew's own blood kin, ain't she?"

"She is. The thing I keep wondering is who would go against us? Who is trying to take Adeline away?"

"That Judge what done sent them down to the Police station I'm thinking," Hattie's indignant reply rang through the room. "You want I put my nephews on this to find out who be causin' trouble?"

"No, Hattie, the situation might reverse and we don't want those boys in a jail cell, too."

"It won't be the first time, but you right. They trying to live according to the law and what we got all this time, our very own in the highest places lyin' and cheatin' and callin' each other names? It ain't right."

"My husband and I knew this Judge when he was young and thought he would make a difference."

Hattie just shook her head, reaching out finally to grasp Harriet's hand. "We don wanna lose our babies."

"I've done all I can," Harriet replied. "But in all truth it doesn't feel enough, that nice young man I remember my husband helping has turned into a man in someone's pocket and has blood in his eye."

The phone rang and Harriet left Hattie dusting while she took the call in the study. "Harriet Becker," she answered. A voice said," Mrs. Becker, you are messing with the wrong people. It would be a shame if your house burned to the ground. The house your fine upstanding husband built to showcase your beauty. Maybe you should take a second thought as to what you are getting yourself into."

Almost immediately the phone rang again. "Harriet, this is Judge Springer."

"Hello Fitch, you don't mind if I don't call you Judge, do you?"

"No, Harriet, I know who I am."

"Yes, you began your journey as a nice young man who had a problem, as I recall, and my husband came to your aid."

"Let it go, Harriet. Now, I'll tell you what I can do. The Graves stay in jail until court date. The children remain housed with their friends, since they are settled in and content but I do understand there has been a request to allow them to stay in their own home under temporary guardianship."

"I'm not happy about this Fitch, and my attorney's will be working on it, but for now we will accept."

*　*　*　*　*　*　*

An associate of Harmon, Butler and Lane placed the last three letters on the sign before adhering to the glass front window. 'You did well," the black haired lady said to Butler. "We have to be able to verify our standing in the community and that should do it."

"Aunt Lane," the young man replied, "How did you get caught up in this? It almost has the ring of a case we have all been told to stir clear of."

Amelia Lane chuckled. "Money made it easy. When a woman wants a baby she goes to great extremes."

"Will I meet this client?"

"As a matter of fact you will. She will be bringing in the third payment this morning."

"So that's how it works." Butler whistled low. "It's all about the money. If you have enough, someone will help you."

"Specifically the law firm of Harmon, Butler and Lane," Amelia laughed, taking a gold slim line case from her purse, to produce a white cigarette. "It's regrettable Harmon has quit smoking, now he insists I do so in the snack room, so our clients won't feel uncomfortable when they aren't allowed to either." She flicked a matching lighter into action and pulled a draw. "Ah, I feel it all ready. I'm ready for bear."

Nine o'clock closed and the hour for delivery was on. Precisely as the clock struck ten, Britany walked in. Opening her purse to produce a zippered bag, her eyes then latched on Marcus Butler. "I have an appointment with Miss Amelia Lane."

Evidently, Butler was thinking, the lady had visited the office before. Glancing around the room, she then chose the plush executive chair Amelia normally sat in. Sitting quite crisp, her legs crossed, hands folded in her lap, she spoke, "Tell Amelia not to take too long because I have another appointment."

From the snack room, Amelia came, artificial smile slashed across her face as she extended a hand to Britany. "Good to see you, Britany." Amelia's eyes betrayed her animosity to Britany in her chair. "I see you prefer my chair."

"I came to collect the child." She had no other reason to drive in from the farm so early. "You have two installments. What is the hold up?" Her voice became clipped, near demanding. "Where is the child?"

"There's a reason the child is not here. The mother will not sign her over but that's really not a problem. Just bear with me. We need to take our time, so as to rile no one and then Adeline will be yours."

Britany glanced at her watch. "Must I remind you, you promised the child would be in my arms. I could slip away unnoticed and that would be the beginning and end of my adopting Summer Walden's child." She arose from the chair. "Did I fail to give you enough money? It seemed to me the stakes were high."

"That's cold, Britany, but then you've always been this way, cold and spoiled, considering only you."

"And you have always been willing to share any money I was willing to hand out. Bring the child to me." Britany slung the leopard scarf over her shoulder and walked out. "Why I ever considered ours a friendship, I'll never know." Turning, she reclaimed the zippered bag, her eyes daring reprisal.

"No, you won't, Britany. It takes being a friend to have one. You will never grow up to face the truth."

Butler returned as quickly as the door closed. "What's the connection between that woman and the Walden's?"

Amelia gave a disgruntled laugh. "It's deep. Walden slept with Summer, his step daughter. Eventually, Summer moved on to Andrew Graves. Walden was furious and became careless, that's when Summer accused her mother of allowing her stepfather's sins and advances. Skip to phase two. Walden returned to the small town where he was born and spoiled by his crazy, literally crazy mother…" Amelia remembered something she wasn't sharing, and then continued… "Britany James was practically run out of her home town after an affair with a married man whose wife went after her with a baseball bat and for some reason…oh, yes, the reason was Matt Langley's wife was in charge of re-furbishing the Shining Light Church…Britany wanted Matt Langley but for some ridiculous reason wound up in the throes of Clayton Walden."

"This makes literally no sense to me. What does Britany James wanting Summer Walden's child have to do with anything?"

"I'm not certain." For once, Amelia sank into a chair other than her own. "Blackmail, for one thing. Walden's wife doesn't really want to raise a child, but neither does she want Andrew Graves to have her granddaughter. Along comes Britany who was supposed to have had a baby this spring, whether she did or not, I don't know…but suddenly I'm hearing she wants Summer's child, a ploy to get even with both Walden and his wife for all the illicit acts he did to her, whether drugs or heaven knows what."

She lit another cigarette, enjoying the breaking of rules but most of all the sensation it created in her mind. "I know the Graves are friends with the Langley's. Remember she wanted Matt Langley but that new decorator in town won him hands down. Would she think it would hurt the Langley's if she took their friend's child? This is where it gets beyond my understanding and I thought I'd heard it all by now."

"I think you are missing something. Something has niggled at my mind. The guy Britany James married, isn't he a partner in the law firm with Andrew Graves? Something else comes into play here, doesn't it?"

"If it does, it is so far beyond anything I've took into consideration, I'll never figure it out."

"Maybe they are just cruel people; something went wrong and they don't care who they hurt because they think they're getting even. There are people who carry grudges a lifetime. Given opportunity, would they act?" He sighed, shaking his head. "I've met a few people that fly under that flag."

"So you think some people carry a grudge a lifetime? Do you think revenge is sweet, Butler?" She started to rise, but settled down to hear his answer. "You seem to have thought on this case awhile."

"Perhaps revenge is sweet. If someone ripped your life apart I imagine you'd feel the hurt but I don't know you well enough to know what you'd do." He studied her through squinted eyes. She was a hard one to read, didn't talk about her past but had no qualms in seeing people suffer, whether the reason was their own doing or someone creating cause. He walked around her very carefully and kept his own business to himself. Still, what was her connection to the Walden's and Britany James?"

"I don't understand the Graves woman. She risk all for her husband's love child." Amelia studied the carefully manicured tip of her finger. "There's a reason I never had a kid."

* * * * * * *

It was ten thirty when the phone rang. Harriet was hesitant to answer considering the previous caller. She checked caller ID. "Hello, Jim, are you two back home safe and sound by now?" She had a fondness for her two escorts; she compared their relationship to a grandmother and grandsons. His voice was excited as he began to speak and she listened carefully. "Then, it isn't Walden's wife wanting Addy? But she is Addy's legal grandmother." Jim continued as Harriet's heart lurched and her hand tightened on the phone. "You are sure? Why, Jim? Why would she want our sweet baby girl?"

She was beside her self, the information was stinging and she needed to tell someone but Marigold already suffered from the woman's obsession to take Matt away from her, though now Britany had a husband; that strange named fellow who was partner with Andrew, a handsome fellow who must love Britany a lot to put up with her shenanigans. Harriet dialed Daniel Gates. Oh, how she wished Bitty was alive. "Daniel, I have just learned information relevant to our Adeline. I don't know what to do with it and maybe there's nothing it will help but I want to tell you."

* * * * * * *

"I can't believe what some people will do to hurt another." Daniel shook his head, "I should rephrase that, I can't believe what we humans are capable of doing and yet…" He sighed wearily. "Ellen, come, let's go into the bedroom and discuss this. Aren't you ready to settle down?" Seeing her nod, although she was distracted after Jewel and Evan asked if she could work with them to set their wedding date up, meaning before originally planned, she followed and sit on the end of the bed waiting for him to begin.

"That was Harriet on the phone. Those two guys we see occasionally, that work for her, or either have some kind of life contract to come to her aid, beats me what it is, but they always show up when she needs them."

"What's wrong? Is Harriet sick?" Now he was gaining her attention.

"No, not ill but probably angry. Remember the animosity between Marigold and Britany James, the one who boldly claimed she wanted Matt, as though he had nothing to do with what she wanted?"

"Daniel has Britany done something to Marigold?" He cast a puzzled glance her way. "Well you are beating around the bush. Just spit it out. What's wrong?"

"Harriet's body guards, for a lack of better explanation of their work, discovered and feel one hundred percent sure it is Britany creating the problems of paternity for Adeline. Can you figure that one out?" Daniel paced the floor, door to wall, hands in his pockets jiggling coins. "It's unbelievable but they say true."

"She doesn't think Anne is capable? That's absurd. Anne is a good mother. Who is Britany James to question? Andrew is the child's father."

"Exactly." He was glad to finally feel her exasperation. "But that's not it." Ellen was staring at him. "It is Britany. She expects to win the court case for custody of Adeline with intention to adopt her."

* * * * * * *

"Britany James…whatever her last name is wants to adopt Adeline? You have got to be kidding." Marigold dropped to the kitchen chair, elbows on the table letting them slide as she considered her mother's words. "Who told this to you? She was due to have her own baby last month. Last month."

"I'd understand if it were me, but Andrew and Anne?" Questions were popping into her mind faster than she could comprehend. "Who would know the truth about this?" Putting both hands to her temples she said, "It is hard to think faced with this kind of information. Do they know? Anne and Andrew, do they know?" Now, drumming her fingers on the table top, she answered her own question. "They have to know. They can't lose Adeline." She closed her eyes, to think. "That woman, Black was her last name. I guarantee you she knows. And to think we all thought Adeline's grandmother Walden wanted her and we had such a fear. Did I come to that conclusion on my own, or did you think so too?"

"What's the difference? She will back Britany and there's enough money between the two to get the job done."

"This makes me sick. Maybe now, Matt will understand sweet little Britany really is the spoiled child I have told him, all along, she is." Marigold's eyes were as bright and snappy as her words. Harriet watched her daughter handle this newest situation with Britany. "They are our friends, I am truly sorry they will have to go through this with her. At least Matt was an adult, but to push in on the life of a baby. To think at one point I felt sorry for her and actually made myself believe she needed friendship."

"The question is what can be done about it."

"Andrew's an attorney. Surely he knows." Marigold stopped talking, staring at her mother. "Doesn't he?"

"From what I understand, the whole thing rests on the court date and Judge. It may even be in the Judge's chambers which means no outsiders present, no one's speaking in behalf of Andrew and Anne, and we knew this Judge. He is for the Walden's; therefore he will dredge up Andrew's past."

"Then, as Ellen says, we must pray for a miracle." Marigold collected her purse and rose to leave. "In the meantime we are having a wedding this weekend and I have arrangements to talk over with Jewel. Have you seen her wedding gown? It's beautiful and she made it."

"I've been amazed they would move the date for their wedding in the event they could keep the Graves' children."

"It was Evan's idea." Marigold tilt her head, musing a moment, "Why would a single man do that?"

"He's different. A bit eccentric, a little vulnerable to the point all most backwards," Harriet replied.

"Backwards, huh?" Marigold hugged her mother. "Is that a euphemism or just plain old time talk?"

"I think it's a description of one who lived a sheltered life, maybe even a suppressed life."

CHAPTER 13

Daniel watched Evan polishing the car. Harriet had taken good care of it. He remembered when she purchased the smaller car all on her own and she had done a good job.

"Where do you plan to take your bride, Evan?"

"We discussed Nashville; that way I could drop in on the man who sells my instruments and I do have two to add to the collection. Of course, we'd have to leave a bit earlier." He paused, turning to study Daniel as he took a cloth to polish the front tire. "What bothers us most is that the right to keep Addy and Andy could come in before we returned and that does concerns us."

"They will be with us, Evan, and we aren't going to kick them out. They have adjusted nicely."

Evan smiled. "What's not to adjust to? All of you treat us so good, it's better than what we're used to, the question is, are you and Ellen adjusting to being handed all this...I mean, it has to be a chore."

"It's amazing to watch how God provides, Evan. If Jewel wasn't here to help Ruthie, or vice versa, then it would be difficult but with Ellen filling in for Anne to keep Anne's job and Jewel being an adult we don't worry about the twins all day." Daniel stood, stretched his back and studied what he'd been doing. The wheel sparkled. "They don't make cars like they used to." He grinned, knowing the history of the car. "You know once Harriet drove all over her front yard in this car, chasing a man who had created all kind of havoc to our group's world."

Evan patted the hood of the car. "This thing is like a tank. We ought to fit right in, in Nashville, shouldn't we? Aren't they kind of known for being eccentric?"

"I don't know are country and eccentric the same thing?"

"Sometimes," Evan grinned. "Since I've been here I've been called backward and illiterate."

"You're gaining ground now that you're talking." Daniel gave him a nudge on the back as he passed by. "Anything you need before I leave?"

"Not here and not in a hurry but if you'd come down to Andrew's building, where I'm staying and help me move an object I'd appreciate it. I'd like to finish a job before he comes home."

"What's that?"

"He had all that wood paneling stacked for the walls and I've been finishing it out but I've reached a spot I need a little assistance."

"Why don't we go do that right now and then we won't have to worry about it if we get busy?"

Relief shone on Evan's face. "I am glad you said that, with things up in the air I don't want to do anything to be in Andrew or Anne's way." There was a faraway look in his eye as if he reviewed something from the past.

That night as Daniel helped Ellen clear the table, he said, "Ellen, there's something about Evan we have been missing. That sad look he often wears, I believe is from a sad time. You notice he doesn't speak of his parents and his regard for Jewel's is hard to read."

"You mean disrespect?"

"No, he just doesn't agree with the raising Jewel experienced but I'm not sure his has been better."

"Everyone has a story, Daniel. Look at yours and mine."

"True," he said stepping behind her, his arms around her waist as he settled his chin on her shoulder. "How do you manage to still smell wonderful at the end of the day?"

"It's all those sweet kisses we get when we arrive home from work."

"Is it enough, spending time with them before you start dinner?"

"I think with the girls standing in during the day, I'm having more quality time with them. What do you think?"

"Seems to be working," Dan agreed. "Jewel's influence is good and our sweet Ruthie…you can't beat. When I brought up Evan, I meant to tell you he has done one perfect job on finishing Andrew's Get-a-way. He's a super craftsman. I'd love to see more of the instruments he builds."

"I tell you what, Daddy of the year, help me finish cleaning up here, I need your input on something I've conjured up for Jewel's wedding. Marigold and I are sharing the decorating and that has halved the task. Otherwise, I might have to stay up several nights."

"Conjured, huh?" He tilt his head, his mouth in that quizzical way she was used to when he found something she said or did humorous. "So where does Jewel fit in here? What is she doing?"

"Sewing tiny seed pearls on her dress." Ellen grinned. "And to your next question, she has taught Ruthie and they are deep in pearls."

"I can't believe this, the youngun's asleep in bed, Danny and Sammy watchin' bedtime stories and you and I alone…in the kitchen. Isn't there a better place for us?"

"You bet, big daddy, follow me to the bedroom." He tossed the dish towel on the rack and followed. She opened the door to reveal a bed covered in garlands of roses while to one side a metal arch leaned against the bed posts. She heard him groan. "There's six feet of space in between, isn't that enough?"

"Aww, you're no fun." She poked him in the ribs. He grabbed her hand and pulled her close. "So what's the big question here?" She pointed to the base of the arch where she had made wooden boxes attached to a long board that extended two feet to the back to keep the arch from falling over.

"What do you think?"

"Hon, why didn't you ask me or Evan to take care of this? It will work but you need a couple shims to tighten the arch pole in tighter. I'd say it will do fine." He shook his head. "Next time let me help."

"Tell you what Daddy of the year, help me clear the roses and turn back the spread and we will lay down and you can tell me your day's adventure." She laughed. "And stop that."

He was wiggling his eyebrows Groucho Marx fashion. "I love our busy household," he said as he spread his arms wide.

"Me, too," she replied, falling into his arms. "You will never change, will you?"

"I hope not, I'm the man who's living the dream, my dream; you and the kids."

"We're blessed, but it wasn't always such fun for me. I think I appreciate everything more as I remember what a hard time Ruthie and I had before you come along, but there was Bitty..." She sighed. "Bitty loved us. I miss her, Daniel. Sometimes, I wonder why God takes people we think we need so much."

* * * * * *

"Are you excited?" Ruthie placed the last pearl in Jewel's hand. With two pins sticking out of her mouth as she tacked the thread back of the pearl, Jewel didn't answer but a slow blush had begun climbing its way from her neck up to her cheeks. "I'm excited," Ruthie exclaimed. "Your dress is beautiful and I think every day you are becoming more pretty than the day before. You look like a princess."

"I second that." Evan came from behind. Jewel must have heard him stepping down the hall; already she had thrown a light sheet over her dress. "I thought you had finished your dress."

Standing, Jewel waited a moment for her body to catch up. She had been on her knees for hours. "I finished the dress but I kept thinking about the pearls and finally gave in and started sewing them on."

He reached across to touch her hand. "I'd have loved you in a burlap sack."

"Sorry, we are fresh out of burlap sacks." She sit on the edge of the bed. "Do we need to do anything to your room?" He shook his head. "Do we need to add anything to the car?" Again, he shook his head. "Am I going with you?" Startled, Evan glanced up to give her his full attention.

"What kind of question is that? Of course you are going with me. You aren't trying to back out, are you?" He led her from the room, out into the night on the front porch, where he had sit his violin.

She grinned. "I'm just tired. Aren't you?" Ruthie was creeping away, trying to go unnoticed.

"I've never had a wife. I find it rather interesting to think I can see you every hour, ask how you are and care for you."

"That's sweet," she replied. "I imagine us sitting at the table, walking down the road hand in hand."

"I've never slept in the same bed with anyone, before," Evan said quietly. "Do you stay on your side?"

"I can." For a moment she wondered…"Is that what you want?"

"No. I want you right here." He tapped his right arm with the left. "I want to hold you close. I've never had anyone really close to me."

"Your body or your heart?" She asked, softly. Their eyes were locked on each other.

"Neither." He answered, dropping his head. "I always wondered what it would be like to be held."

"Didn't your mother hold you?"

"No, I think she wanted to but there was this stubbornness that wouldn't let her." Reluctantly, he sat on the low stool they had brought in to lay the gown on. "I have something to tell you. So you won't think she's a cold woman." He sighed, picking up a jar of buttons, wondering where they came from. "The woman I call mother isn't really my mother. She was very ill one winter and they thought she was dying. I think it was some disease plus pneumonia which nearly was her end. My father, her husband, in his despair, drank until he was drunk. Her sister was there and he invited her to join him. They thought she was dying, you understand?" Jewel nodded. "The wrong thing happened between them. Months later as Abagail, who is my father's wife, was recovering; her sister came up pregnant with my father's child. Me."

Jewel reached to put her hands on his shoulders as she sank to her knees before him, staring into his eyes as she listened. "They were ashamed and embarrassed. The sister stayed on to deliver her child hoping no one would ever know but she died giving birth to me and my father's wife raised me as her own but my father's indiscretion had put a wedge between them. She could not believe while she was deathly ill such a thing could happen and he could not convince her it was because he was drunk and that he put no significance to the act."

"How sad." From her own small community Jewel remembered gossip and separation of families. "We must promise each other we will do our best to honor God's word, his commandments, to stay together." Letting her arms slip around his neck, she lay her head on his shoulder. "We must learn to love. I have always wondered if my parents truly love each other or if it is only a marriage where they work together to survive."

"What do you want, Jewel?" He spoke quietly, as though the answer was of utmost importance.

"Laughter from our lips and joy in our heart," She whispered. "Christmas with happiness, Easter with peace."

"I will try to give you that." Evan's eyes shone with love. "We will build a wonderful life together."

She studied him, grateful for his goodness, his serious charm. "I will hold you, Evan, and never let go."

"Yes. Hold me the rest of our life, Jewel. I have waited for you, knowing something was missing but like Jesus love, I did not know what it was." They arose together and he leaned to kiss her cheek. "I may not see you tomorrow. Daniel and I are making sure the garden is perfect."

"Ruthie and I are watching the children, as usual, but we are also making punch and tiny little cupcakes to ice in white frosting. Ellen has collected beautiful little cups for the punch and matching plates." She sighed with contentment. "I am so happy."

"Sit in Ellen's swing, I have something for you." He took the violin from the case. "Tell me if you recognize the song." He drew the bow against the strings and began the melody he held in his heart, every note sharing with Jewel the story they longed to tell. "I come to the garden alone, while the dew is still on the roses, and the voice I hear…calling on my ear, the Son of God discloses….and I walk with Him and I talk with Him none other…" He heard her singing and from the house, Dan and Ellen's voice joined in. "It will be hard to leave this place," he whispered. As in agreement, two lightening bugs floated by, a light in the darkness. In the next hour, Evan walked home to Andrew's Get-A-Way, his heart filled with gladness. He had lived for this hour until he and Jewel stood before Pastor Joe to say their vows. Time had seen him wondering about the emptiness of life. Amazed, his step quickened; how often do we live a lifetime for a moment's revelation, he wondered, "For this I was born."

* * * * * *

Studying the thin gold case, she tossed her black hair feeling the swish of strands across her shoulder. She had worked hard to keep the persona Clayton said he loved about her. It wasn't easy keeping the pounds off as she aged, but for him she tried her utmost. She had died to her family. They never accepted him, thinking he was crude, self-centered and ruthless and he was. That's what she loved about him. Then the trickle of other women began. She could forgive him having a wife but not them.

Some said there was no way he could have died in last summer's debacle. She remembered laughing at the newspapers account, thinking he's too smart to get caught up in something so ridiculous. It was a Star Wars fiasco. But when she didn't hear from him, she began to wonder if it were true he died. This morning she awakened with Summer Walden's child on her mind. His wife wanted the child in order to get rid of the reminder her husband had been unfaithful with her daughter. Britany James wanted the child to replace the one she lost. Something was funny about that story, too.

Amelia considered Butler. Dumbstruck, Butler believed everything she told him and a plan was forming in her head, one she couldn't press down, it was forming on its own but she needed another person to help her push it through. She could not be here and there. Unbuttoning her blouse another two buttons she strolled into the office, knowing Butler would be waiting.

"Good morning," Smiling benevolently she slid upon the desk, leaving her skirt pressed high, to reveal without hosiery those long beauties she pampered for Clayton's return. She realized Butler was swallowing and trying to adjust to the moment. "Beautiful morning, isn't it?"

He handed a paper to her. "Here's the report you wanted."

She read the last line. "The child is presently with the Graves family, has settled in without problems."

* * * * * *

THE WEDDING

Ruthie was beautiful in her poufy white dress. Bitty had found the dress in one of the down town shops and bought it knowing years would pass before it fit Ruthie. She reminded Ruthie and Ellen the dress needed to be hung in Ruthie's closet. "One day, Ruthie will need a special dress and there it will hang."

It was as she said. Tears slid down both their cheeks thinking of Bitty, but Ruthie tried on the dress and smiles replaced the tears. "It fits perfect," Ruthie chimed while Ellen said, "You look beautiful, Sweetums."

"Jewel really likes this dress." Ruthie whirled around, letting the dress fall back into its original position.

"What's not to like?" Daniel leaned down to kiss her cheek. "You aren't getting married, too, are you?"

"Oh, Daddy, you know I'm too young. I'm the flower girl for Jewel and Evan's wedding."

He clicked his fingers together. "Oh, that's right; it's not your wedding. I am so glad."

"Jewel's parents have arrived. I left them in the living room; otherwise the boys might attack them." Ellen shuddered. "There's an atmosphere that is not good and if Sammy and Danny felt it, oh, my…"

"Who's watching them?" Daniel straightened his tie and headed for the door. "I think I'm it."

"Evan has no family, Momma. Isn't that sad?" Ruthie watched as Ellen finished dressing Holly and Noel. Both were asleep as she slipped them into the dress up clothes they wore on Easter Sunday. "But his friends from church will sit on his side."

"What about Jewel's friends?"

"She wasn't allowed many friends, Momma. Her parents considered their being together a waste of time but she still has a few from her church, too." Ruthie thought for a minute and then confided, "I really like Jewel, Momma, and she says I'm easy to talk to, but her parents have been really strict."

"They won't stop the wedding. Will they?" Ellen straightened and stretched her back. "I'm glad we don't have too many of these fancy gatherings," she grinned at Ruthie and pinched her nose. "My stretcher wasn't stretching as well as it used to, changing the twins diapers. Sometimes, I'm just plain ole tired." Ellen started out of the room and stopped, "you didn't answer my question, does Jewel expect any trouble?" Ruthie shook her head. "Good," Ellen hugged her daughter. "I don't need any excitement. Do you?"

Except for the one time when Pastor Joe ask the question, if anyone finds this couple should not be united in matrimony, the wedding went smoothly, please stand, he said and Jewel's mother stood but Jewel's father pulled her back down to the seat, all the while shaking his head vehemently. Ruthie had dropped flower petals down the path in front of Jewel while Ellen played the piano but the highlight was when Evan played the violin he had made and every heart yearned for the love they were feeling to last forever.

"It was a beautiful ceremony, Ellen," Harriet said. "and Evan's talent blessed us more than he can ever know. It was a sweet part if the ceremony when he played the violin."

"They're gone." Ruthie burst into the room. "In your car, Nana, didn't you want them to leave it here?"

"What else would they drive, Ruthie?" Harriet stooped to look into Ruthie's face, "What else?"

"Horses and a carriage," Ruthie giggled. "But that would be slow."

"I saw the love in their eyes and I feel good about their marrying. I take it, there has been very little show of emotion, thus far, and I do wonder how long that can last?" Harriet chuckled. "We are going to see a change."

"Can you turn them into a prince and princess, Nana?" Harriet just shook her head, on her way to see the happy couple before they drove out of sight. Instead, she saw trouble walking up the driveway. 'Oh, no. Ruthie go stay in the room with our sweetheart, that woman is back, the one who wants our baby."

With a court order in hand, Amelia handled the transfer of baby Adeline to her car, oblivious to either the baby's cries or Anne's. "We were friends with her mother." Adeline's mother," Anne wailed.. "But I can't know what's legal or not until Andrew can tell me."

CHAPTER 14

"You have driven in Memphis before, Evan?" Jewel was studying the map.

"No, I haven't but I Daniel gave me directions to the hotel and there's a shop in the hotel he says I must visit."

"I can't believe any of today has actually happened. You don't have to impress me, Evan."

He smiled. "Actually, all the people involved with the wedding wanted to impress you. Harriet's gift besides the car was where we would stay tonight." He glanced her way. "She said you would be delighted with the history."

Laughing, Jewel clapped her hands together. "I won't ask."

"It was hard leaving the little ones, wasn't it?"

Immediately Jewel covered her face with her hands. "I felt like crying, I've become so attached to them."

"They are in the best of hands," he replied. They crossed the Mississippi river and made the turn Daniel designated on the map. "From here on, he says it's clear sailing. We will be there shortly." And they were. "On the outside it looks like a regular place, doesn't it?" The porters came immediately to take their luggage; waiting just long enough for Evan to realize they expected a tip. "Now that concerns me," he wore a quimsical expression. "I don't know what they expect and I feel concerned leaving Harriet's car. Those guys looked at it like it was a train or something in the wrong place."

Jewel's joy was expanding. "We are at a grand place, aren't we?" She reached for Evan's hand. "If they do their research and see the car is worth money that will change their tune. Besides, Miss Harriet gave the car to you, didn't she?"

"That left me in a blind spot too, but yes, she did."

Entering the lobby of the hotel was a picture of opulence. In the center of the room, was a fountain. "Oh, Evan, I can't believe this." Jewel pinched her arm to show him. Evan stooped to kiss the spot.

"Third floor," the lady behind the mahogany divider said, "Room three thirteen."

"I assume it is all right if I carry you across the threshold of room three thirteen," Evan whispered, "Our first night as husband and wife, I have to, I hear that puts a blessing on our marriage."

"Are you that couple?" They turned to stare at the lady who had dismissed them. "From Missouri?" They nodded. "Oh, my, come with me, your friend would have me fired if I forgot her instructions. We have a special room for you." At her insistence they followed, "This," she said with a wide sweep of her hand as she opened the door, "is our special room for special people, not just the wedding suite but the celebration suite for wonderful significant happenings in lives." She was agile as a flying fairy sweeping around the room touching items, pouring liquid drink into beautiful crystal glasses, stopping at last to finish, "As I understand you are newlyweds. Your friend reminded us you are not even social drinkers, thus you have chilled white grape of elixir in your glass. Now I must be on my way. Everything's free. Enjoy. Enjoy! We hope you will remember us always. Ta-ta."

"Was she real?" Evan was holding her hand, guiding her back out into the hall. His laughter joined hers as he stooped, picked her up into his arms and crossed into the suite Harriet had reserved for them.

* * * * * *

They awoke to the gentle patter of rain on the window glass. "It's not supposed to rain on our special day," he said, but he was grinning. "I'm hungry, are you hungry?" She nodded. "We can eat in," Evan said, pulling Jewel into his arms. "Or, we can check out that fabulous restaurant that serves breakfast that Harriet has on her list." He kissed Jewel on the forehead, liking the feel of her body in his arms, her head resting against his shoulder. "I dreamed of having someone to love me all my life." He sighed a healthy thankful sigh, "I'll tell you how forlorn my early life was if you promise not to cry."

"I'll try not to cry, but I'm so happy my emotions are riding on my sleeve."

"Then up, up, up, here we go…get dressed and we will check out Harriet's description of "wonderful food." Evan picked up the letter the welcoming lady had given them saying it was from their benefactor. "I've never known such kindness, Jewel. Why would she bless a stranger such as I?"

"Two strangers," Jewel replied. "That is what we have encountered, people who love God and us." She kissed him sound on the lips ready to put on day clothes. "Let's explore, Evan, to see what's out there."

Evan called front desk asking them to deliver their car to the street next to the restaurant. A few minutes later a knock on the door confirmed the task done as the keys were placed in Evan's hand. Out the lobby doors, onto the street, they were entering the restaurant when Evan halted. "Jewel?" His voice was punctuated by shock. "Jewel, is that Addy? Look to your right, the man in line holding her in his arms, "Why would our Addy be in Memphis when she is supposed to be with the Gates until court date where you and I have signed an agreement to be there for her and look there's her stroller."

Sensing Jewel was about to move forward, Evan put a hand on her arm. "Wait," he whispered, "Something isn't right, the black haired lady at the counter…isn't that Ms. Amelia or whatever her name that came to the Gates house to take Addy away? That is definitely our Addy."

"I cannot bear this, our Addy in a stranger's arms." Jewel once more felt the constraints of his hand. "Please, Evan, something is wrong. We need to take Addy from them."

"I'm afraid there will be the other two, also, Jewel. The two men who came …we have to be careful."

"We are going to take her away from them, aren't we?" Jewel's eyes filled with tears. "Is Addy asleep?"

"Or drugged," he guessed. "Jewel, whichever of us has hold of Addy, go to the car, start it. Don't worry right off putting her in her car seat, just be ready to drive away. Even if we are separated, Jewel, get in the car and head to Missouri. You drove your parents, right?" She nodded. "This is serious, Jewel, in the short time we left they have stolen Addy, now we must return her. Take the keys to the car."

"Why haven't the Gates alerted us, Evan?"

Taking out his cell, Evan scanned. "There it is Jewel, let me read it." Evan and Jewel, we are terribly upset. The court has somehow finagled custody of Adeline and we are hopeless as how to change this. She is not to leave the state for any reason until true guardianship is established. We are worried."

"Tennessee is another state," burst from their lips. "Something is definitely wrong." Glancing toward the man holding the baby, they saw him leaving the baby in the stroller by the rest room door and the black haired lady was not in sight. "Go start the car Jewel." Evan was already moving toward the baby.

Jewel was on the street, finding the car to slide behind the steering wheel. Fumbling, she managed to put the key in the ignition, backed out of the parking place and turned toward Evan coming through the door with a sleeping baby on his shoulder. "Go," he shouted as he climbed into the front seat. "And don't let up."

"Is she all right, Evan. No crying or movement. I can't bear this. Tell me Evan…"

"Go Jewel, we have no time to lose. They will miss the baby and come after us."

Making a right turn on river drive, they were soon on the bridge, traffic heavy and no one lingering with West Memphis coming up next and then their turn on to Interstate Fifty Five. Harriet Becker's car performing like the stack of steel it was made of, Jewel had time to reflect on her parent's way of slow driving and was immediately glad the friend who had lived down the road had a race track complete with dune buggies they sped around in building skills. She had never told her parents since it was in the rear of the family's private woods. They would have forbidden her going to the neighbor's home.

Sweat had formed on Evan's brow as now he was uncovering Addie to see why she was asleep. He called her name. "Adeline." Groggy, she opened her eyes for a second but they closed shut again. "Jewel, I can't explain what I'm feeling but in my heart, meeting this little girl shined light on my frugal existence in a way I'd never known or ever expected to experience. The woman who lived as my mother would never bend for my sake or hers and I suppose I carried that cold hardness around inside of me, wondering how one could do that when surely there was more to love and sharing and caring about each other, then after all these years I meet baby Adeline, Anne must have shoved her off into my arms for some reason…and when she did I felt this overwhelming love for this child I barely knew, in a room full of believers willing to lay low and let me find my way. I'm just saying perhaps my moment of fame that everyone should experience…mine may not be large but a revelation to my heart and soul that a child could care and recognize a good trait in me, for I feel that Adeline did just that. He thought for a minute, "She will come out of it," he gave a deep sigh of relief. "I don't really know what to do now, Jewel. If the authorities allowed her to be taken from the state, who do we trust?"

"Maybe we are to keep to the speed limit and not do anything to attract attention." Quickly she glanced his way. "But then, how do we go back into the Cape to the Gates?"

"I don't know, but it's Anne and Andrew I'm thinking are concerned beyond themselves." Evan's brow was wrinkled with worry. "Since we've been with these families, who are all friends, I have heard Miss Harriet has people that protect her and no one knows why. Do you think she could help us out of this dilemma?" Jewel could only nod, they were desperate. "Then I'll call her and explain our predicament."

Jewel listened as the two phones connected and Evan explained their situation to Harriet Becker. He left the phone on speaker for Jewel to hear. "Evan, we are so distraught our baby girl being taken from the family, I feel sure we can correct this problem. I will make contact with my people and according to your own words you will arrive at the Cape within two hours if nothing goes wrong. My friends will be driving a black sedan with windows tinted only to the degree allowed by law but they will bring you safely to my home. I will call an old friend to back me up in the wisdom of our actions. Be careful and don't stop for anything. The less people see you the better we will handle this situation."

"How does she do this, Evan? Where did she get such authority?"

"I've never heard of her doing anything wrong, Jewel. I think she has the finances to back her plans and in today's world that speaks volumes, then too, she seems to have influential friends. Wouldn't that help?" Holding Adeline closer, he kissed the top of the baby's head. "I have to put her in the car seat. We must not be stopped for the reason of putting her in danger."

* * * * * *

They neared the seventy seventh mile marker, the blood running through their veins felt like ice water as they felt their bodies stiffen from stress in not knowing what to expect. When two cars emerged as if from out of thin air, Jewel sat up straighter at the wheel and Evan pretended to be sound asleep on the passenger side. "It's two black cars, Evan, with darkened windows. One is behind us, the other immediately across from me, side by side."

"I'll call Miss Harriet and ask her if they can give us a signal so we will know for certain it is them." He made the call. "She said she would call them to put on their emergency flasher and then we will know." Within five minutes both black cars gave signal and the three cars entered the Cape. The first car led, pulling away as they arrived at Harriet's drive, followed by the one behind Harriet's car. The security gate to the garage entrance opened and Jewel drove inside. Once the door was down to the garage, Evan and Jewel left the car with baby Adeline secure in Evan's arms.

Harriet stood in the doorway, her arms opened wide to receive Adeline. "Thank you, Jesus," she whispered, closing the door securely. "Here you are safe in our arms and I can't tell the Gates or the Graves because the fewer know where you are the safer you will be." She glanced quickly to Evan and Jewel. "We don't know who we can trust." Clasping Adeline to her breast, Harriet was preparing to sit when the door burst open. Two men, resembling those accompanying the lady lawyer when they first thought to take the child into custody, were coming on strong through the door. Old Jeb, the gardener was used as a body shield until they assured themselves opposition was not present. One rap on the head with a gun and old Jeb folded to the floor.

"We will take the baby, now, Mrs. Becker. You've cost us time and money. Our boss lady had someone ready to take the child. You have cost us precious time. For every hour they are deducting a hefty sum."

Harriet stood defiance on her face. "The only way you will take her is over my dead body."

"Suit yourself, old lady," the man moved quickly, slapping angrily at Harriet who eluded him but Evan moved in as a gun went off and Evan staggered, his arms flailing as he tried to gain purchase of any object that would prevent his falling. The gunman gaped at Evan and then his partner. "I never meant to," his face was changing colors as he thought to try to run, seeing his partner was already leaving.

"You stupid jerk," he was hollering back at his partner, "nothings worth our going to prison over this."

Jewel was on the floor beside Evan, her hands beneath Evan's head, trying to straighten him from the fall. "Oh, Evan, Evan, Evan," she kept calling his name. Harriet was calling nine one one, and then her private line to the two who had intercepted Jewel on the high way and led them to her home. Jewel heard her say, "yes, the same car as before, they have shot Evan. I'm sorry I let you go but I had no idea they would trick the yard man and come in the back way."

"The ambulance will be here, soon, Jewel." Harriet clasp Adeline closer to her body. Already a plan was forming in her mind. "It's not fair you are not with your parents, Adeline," she crooned. "Let's see if we can make that happen." Hearing the ambulance's siren, Harriet said, "Jewel, I must take baby Adeline into the back room; let them believe this was a robbery so they won't take her away from us."

The front of Jewel's blouse was wet where tears had landed as she held Evan's head between her hands while blood stained the front of his shirt. Distraught, Jewel said, "I think he's dying, Miss Harriet."

"Don't say that, Jewel, we must not give up hope." She heard the knock at the door and called "Come in." The EMT's came carrying only one bag and the transfer board between them. They accessed the situation, and then loaded Evan on the spinal board ready to take him to Emerson Hospital. Jewel had thrown herself on their mercy and was allowed to ride beside her husband.

Harriet was hard pressed in knowing what to do. Adeline must be protected and how could she do that if they already knew something had happened to Evan or perhaps they could shed light on why they always went after the Gates group of friends. She needed help and needed it now. As Marigold came through the door questioning the disarray she had found in the garage, Harriet was calling the other two she could count on to love Adeline and help her figure out what must be done.

"Ma?" Marigold stood staring at blood on the carpet, exactly where Evan laid. "Ma, what's been happening? It almost looks as though a murder has been committed."

Harriet's hands automatically went to her face as she burst into tears. "I didn't realize how scared I've been. Placing a hand on her daughter Harriet turned toward the bedroom where she'd hidden Adeline. "Come with me. I need to know what you think."

"Ma," Marigold stopped following her mother. "I'm worried at what I'm seeing. Tell me who you hurt?"

"It's not me." Harriet was almost belligerent. "Come to the bedroom with me, now."

"You don't have to snap at me. I'm right behind you." She opened the door and tip-toed in.

"A baby?" Marigold hissed. "What are you doing with someone's baby. You'll go to jail."

"Must I slap you to bring you to your senses? Look at the child, she's a toddler. Who is it?"

"Oh, my word. It's Addy. What did you do with the body? It was Amelia wasn't it?" Now Marigold began to chuckle, letting the laughter build to the point it drift outside. "Mom, how did you pull this one off?" Marigold was beaming. "I couldn't believe they'd lost

Adeline but when I heard you were involved, Oh, Ma," Marigold threw her arms around Harriet, "You've done good."

Harriet heard the doorbell ring and then a certain type of pounding. "That has to be the Gates," she said.

"I'll let them in. You just stay put." Marigold was gone only a few minutes to return with Ellen and Daniel. "I didn't tell them our dilemma, Ma. I thought they would enjoy it as much as I did." The Gates were truly curious as to Harriet sending out a distress signal when she called. "Who's with the kids?" Marigold asked. "I don't think we thought of that."

"Dorothy dropped by," Ellen explained, "hoping there's word on Addy. When Harriet called she insisted she sit with our children and here we are. So what is it needs immediate attention?"

Marigold led them into the bedroom where Addy was hidden beneath the quilt, all except her head and fingertips. "Meet our baby…and then tell us how to keep this child and stay legal since the law office was able to carry out their plan of kidnapping Adeline. "Glancing at the two, Marigold saw they hadn't caught on, yet. "Really, doesn't anything here ring a bell? How about if I remove the hat?"

"Oh, my goodness, how in the world have you accomplished this? We have been scared some little bump in the road would get on the kidnappers nerves and they would treat Addy badly." Stooping over the sleeping child, Ellen folded her into her arms. "I can't tell you how used to holding her I become. Ah, there she is, Daniel. Hi, sweetheart." Addy yawned and stretched. "She doesn't appear much for the worse in her absence from us. Does she?"

"Now we have to give you the bad news. I don't think you've heard." Dan gave her a sharp glance as she continued. "It was Jewel and Evan stumbled onto the people who had Addy in possession. They moved quickly to take her from them and raced back here as quickly as possible. But those people made their way here…Evan was shot and has been taken to Emerson hospital. We don't know anything about his condition. Harriet said Jewel panicked and thought he was dead so it is very serious."

"We should go there to be with Jewel," Dan offered, "But what about our kids," his voice lost the enthusiasm. "You drop me off, back home, and you can check on Jewel. She'll understand."

"I'm amazed," Ellen replied. "There was no way this would normally happen, It is truly a God thing."

"Yes, it is," Harriet agreed. "Otherwise once crooked Amelia reached the people she was selling our baby to, we would never have seen her again. The people could have been from another country."

"And no one alerted the police, not even Amelia?" Concern underlined Daniel's words. "You don't know, do you? Be that as it may, I doubt they can legally pursue her whereabouts." He started for the door, "We need to hurry, Ellen, if things are on the quiet as it seems, Jewel may need someone with her." He shook his head, "To think the Graves have no idea Addy is back, or what happened to Evan."

"Wait up." Marigold was running after them. "Harriet and I agree you need to be with Ellen, Dan. I will go relieve Dorothy and you two please, let me know how things are going time to time. Matt will be in from the farm and Harriet will bring our two over unless she decides to keep them here with Adeline." She was quiet thinking for a moment. "It is a hunch, only, mind you, but I believe Harriet is considering something that usually involves those two that seem to come from nowhere and save the world, if you know what I mean. So let's pray for her, and them, too. Honest to goodness, she does have connections."

"Strange," Ellen mused, "We were beginning to be depressed over Addie's whereabouts, and think our prayers were going nowhere, but God was working it out, except now Evan is hurt and again, only God knows the answer and we must keep our prayers going. For all we've all been through, God is revealing He is still in control. Bless his Holy name."

* * * * * * *

Jewel glanced up to see Dan and Ellen's arrival. She ran to them but having no rest since arriving to the hospital her own strength was diminishing; even as they opened their arms to receive her Jewel went down. "Easy. Easy," Dan was struggling to keep her off the floor. "There you go, Jewel," he was guiding her to the nearest chair. Snuffing, Jewel stifled a cry. "It's all right, Jewel, you're going to be all right."

"I am so scared. They've run test after test on Evan trying to determine if he's slipped into comma or possibly brain dead." Jewel shook so hard she could hardly speak. "There are questions I don't know how to answer."

"We came to sit with you, Jewel. We realize this is difficult. What can I get for you to eat?" Jewel seemed not to comprehend his words. "Eat or drink," Daniel repeated, to which Jewel replied shaking her head no.

"I can't have any distractions," she said, "the doctor said they would be in to explain what they really know." Jewel had only finished speaking when two doctors and a nurse entered the room. "How is he?" The question popped out of her mouth before she realized it. "I mean, has he opened his eyes?"

"Dr. Cameron, Nurse Hayden and I'm Dr. Beale," the doctor introduced himself and the others and shook hands all around. "No ma'am, he is battling this incident in darkness, but it is my opinion rather than coma your husband went into shock. Probably the bleeding began immediately and with the bullet passing through both lungs the bleeding was extensive. Well, we feel it was. He has a double pneumo/hemothorax, caused when the air came through the holes the bullet made which caused the lung to collapse because it could no longer expand and the blood was filling up."

"Do patients recover from double gunshot wounds such as this?"

"Survival rates are poorer when both lungs are injured." He seemed to hesitate, "under good conditions it takes one to three months."

"To live or die," Jewel questioned.

"Either," he replied.

"This is not good news, is it?" Jewel's voice dropped to a hoarse whisper.

"No, young lady, it is not."

* * * * * *

She watched them file in, friends to Daniel and Ellen, taking seats quietly to sit their hands pressed together, some with small bible produced from pockets of shirts or women's purses, and she felt in a stupor trying to sort out what had happened. They had found Addy in Memphis, knowing Daniel said she was not to be taken from the state. She and Evan had reacted simultaneously; their one thought was to rescue Addy. Now that her heart was settling, she couldn't believe they had been so quick to jump to action for the baby's safety. What if they had been stopped, they could have been held for kidnapping. But they weren't, instead they made it back to the Cape and Evan was shot.

They were in a circle now, the friends. She had written an essay on friendship once, and made an excellent grade but the essay was not truth, it was fiction built purely upon the desire to have friends and yet, these people seemed to possess the characteristics she had described. Daniel was praying, the people were murmuring prayers while he prayed, asking God to spare Evan and a young woman was watching her. She came to sit beside Jewel, holding out her hand to be taken and held as long as needed. "Haley?" The young woman nodded and reached over to hug her.

"I was at Mother and Dad's. They said they must come to the hospital for you and your husband. I hope you don't mind I came along?" Jewel whispered thank you. "Jewel, this group has been through some harrowing situations and the one thing I can tell you is you will draw strength as they sit quietly and pray. Right now I'm incapable of doing anything active but I can sit with you and listen if you want to talk." A gentle smile crossed Haley's face as she beckoned someone near. "Come sit with us, Ruthie, with you on one side and me on the other I think Jewel's fear will be replaced by hope."

Later, Marigold drew Haley to one side. "How do you think Jewel is, presently, and how are you?"

"Seriously, Marigold," Haley tilt her head, trying to find the right words, "I think she is still in a state of shock and who am I to say that? But when Ruthie sit beside her and held her hand I saw a settling of the spirit begin. Ruthie has that effect on people, you know. When I was troubled, Ruthie helped me find God and even if Jewel is the best Christian in the world right now her world is turned upside down and she has to find her way through this valley that has been thrust upon her."

Ellen had joined them while Haley was speaking. "Yea, though I walk through the valley of death, thou art with me," she quoted. "I agree, Haley, Evan is alive but he is hovering on the brink and it can go either way. We must all stay strong in our prayers for both of them." She gave the two a hug, "And how are you, Haley? Are you at peace?"

"I am," Haley replied. "I've given God the praise and honor, but I can't say it came easy because I was angry and resentful many times; I had tried so hard to do right with my husband and then the unthinkable happened and to tell Jeremy, our world would fall apart and I don't know if we are strong enough to last through the storm. I believe Psalm twenty three but I decided the truth will go to the grave with me…I love my husband that much that I hope by my actions he always has his father."

Ellen kissed Haley on the cheek, "you are a strong sister," she said, smiling. "We are sister's in Christ and I'll have to tell you our friendship has blessed me many times over. I pray Jewel stays close to the group. She and Evan are younger but their interest and desire to follow the Lord brings us all together."

"This simply is not good, is it, Ellen." Marigold's eyes were dark with concern. "Do we decide one of us should stay with Jewel or will the hospital send us home, anyway? It would be terrible if Evan should die and she was here alone."

"Why don't we find out what Jewel wants."

CHAPTER 15

"We must leave," Daniel explained. "Call any time of the night if you need us and one of us will be here. But for now the children have bedtime hours." Ellen kissed Jewel on the cheek and hugged her firmly. *It was* Ruthie putting her arms around Jewel, forehead to forehead and whispering words of comfort and faith that put a new spark in Jewel's eyes. The next hour when she went in to see Evan she didn't cry.

"I don't know how to handle this, Evan, if you should die. I sit there, in the waiting room and wonder if God plans to take you home when we have just found each other. We both just want to belong to someone. Your loving me may be what propels me to do those things foreign to me that will help me along the way. I've been so hesitant, Evan, because I've lived a sheltered life. I don't know why my parents shied away from others or why they were harsh in judgement. I only know you and I were going to do life a different way. Please stay with me. Please don't die."

Harriet heard Jewel's prayer and turned to allow her privacy to talk to Evan or God as she chose. She had waited until Marigold collected her children to come to the hospital though Hattie assured her she would take good care of them. Remembering the turmoil of her own life in those days when she was rejected by the man who was father of the child she was carrying and the feeling of being lost, unloved and completely alone, she had come to spend time with Jewel who must feel the same, though she was not rejected but possibly facing giving up the love of her life.

Evan had scored a place in Harriet's own heart, in so short a time, she mused. Something about him was endearing, his courteous ways, the quietness of his being; you knew he was present but detached from the personal conversations flowing around him when the group was together, and yet he cared about each person. The children, especially Adeline loved him and he seemed to guard her as though he felt something traumatic might happen to her. Now Harriet wondered how coincidental that Evan should stumble upon Adeline being taken from the state and taken from the families who loved her immediately as Andrew's love child from the past.

"It was a God-thing," she whispered. Now God's hand was on them, watching their actions and the sincerity, no doubt. She watched Jewel leaving Evan's unit, head down and defeated she returned to the sitting area where she had left a few possessions. "Jewel," Harriet spoke. "I've come to sit with you."

"Oh, Miss Harriet, I feel so helpless to do anything for Evan." Tears filled her eyes to run down her cheeks. "Thank you for coming, but it is just draining to sit in this place where hope is all we have." She slid into the chair next to Harriet. "Why would you bother with us, with me, Miss Harriet?"

"You're good people." Harriet reached across to squeeze Jewel's hand. "Believe it or not, I've been through a few of these times of trial and tribulation and I know there's nothing easy about it." She smiled down on the fragile girl beside her. "Sometimes, seeing the face of someone who cares helps."

* * * * * *

The days turned into two weeks, Evan appeared to be sleeping, whatever he was experiencing no one knew, not the doctors or his newly wed wife. Jewel kept vigil, until she asked to speak with the committee of doctors who met weekly to discuss Evan's case and the financial department of the hospital, explaining she had no funds and it would take the rest of her life to pay for Evan's hospital stay, not that she was complaining but she must consider what was to be done for the future.

"We are surprised your husband has lived through the damage to both lungs. Medically he is healing. We have no idea if he hears conversation but we encourage you to talk to him of your hopes and dreams for the future. Perhaps he will respond. We hope he will. As for the monetary worries, the director of finance said you are not to worry; a benefactor who chose to remain anonymous has arranged to pay for your husband's hospital stay."

Jewel was amazed that the group of friends trickled in and out, checking on her, bringing a magazine, a special treat and often tucked beneath the gift would be a love offering of money, sometimes a few dollars and other times a twenty. She was learning the beatitudes of the bible in a profound way. Her parents came in the beginning, frowning and saying, "what have you got yourself into, girl?" Though their harshness brought tears, she could not linger on their attitude when she was blessed by Ruthie coming to visit, young as she was holding Jewel's hand, smiling and whispering Jesus loves you. When Ruthie left Jewel always felt comforted. Perhaps, she thought, a gift of the spirit is merely something the person is willing to share, but then again she realized Ruthie wore a special mantel.

Then came the day Anne and Andrew were to face the Judge. It was common knowledge DNA testing had been done on Andrew. Adeline was his very own. Summer Walden's attorney called on the friends next door to Summer to tell the Judge her desire that Andrew and Anne raise the child. For some reason Clayton Walden's wife did not appear, nor the black haired Amelia and the Judge was not Judge Springer. Unknown to the higher court, the Judge selected to fill in was one and the same the one who demanded Andrew straighten up his act, some ten years previously, once more breathing down his throat, expecting better of one who he always wanted to do his best. There was a day of deliberation and then the Judge declared the case dismissed on grounds that if Andrew Graves was indeed the father as the test declared and the mother of the child had asked Anne Graves to take little Adeline as her own and Anne Graves was in agreement, then why should pundits of the court deem otherwise? What the Judge would never reveal was that his wife was friends with Clayton Walden's wife and to his knowledge though she might pat a child on the head in view of others, she had never wanted one of her own and vowed she would never lower herself to change the dirty diaper of an infant, gross as the act appeared.

The Judge drove home, satisfied he had done the world a favor by keeping the child out of the Walden Family's grip. He wondered how long it would take his wife to put two and two together in regards to the new couple in town that he was actually distantly related to the young man.

Twenty one days later, Ellen was standing at the sink washing dishes, having arrived home from Dr. Lonzo's office where she had promised Anne two weeks at home to settle Adeline and Andy back into their normal routine before returning to be Dr. Lonzo's nurse. She had enjoyed staying busy and learning the older doctor's ways but with Jewel at the hospital by Evan's side and Dorothy doing her best to help with the twins, Ellen knew it was time to return home where she belonged. The phone rang and she hurried to answer, wiping her hands on the nearest towel along the way.

It was Jewel, and her voice was filled with crying. "Ellen, oh, Ellen." There was a pause as she tried to gain control and Ellen's heart felt as though it hit the bottom of her stomach. "Ellen, he's awake. Evan woke up."

"Praise the Lord," Ellen cried out, "you scared me to death. I was afraid he had died."

"You won't believe this, the doctors said that was all they were waiting for, if he passes a few minor test tomorrow, we may go home the next day, that is if Andrew allows us to return to his special place and then, Ellen, when Evan's able we will drive out to his father's land to see if there's entry to it by now."

"Just be cautious. I've heard in some places the water is trapped and a danger. You've made it this far, don't take chances."

"We wouldn't, but isn't it wonderful, Ellen? Evan is awake and would you believe he is hungry."

"I imagine you are, too." Ellen was laughing. "Go find your man a plate and be sure to join him. You both have to stay healthy to help each other and I wouldn't worry about Andrew, he's just a big old bear."

She had heard Daniel enter the house and when she turned he was standing in the door way, waiting. "Is it good news? Because we could use some, don't you think?" He opened his arms and she walked into them, to lay her head on his shoulder. They stood holding each other, no reason to turn loose. As he nuzzled his chin against her hair he asked, "Was it good news?"

"Prayers answered," she replied, looking up to him. "Evan awoke and he's hungry. That's pretty good, isn't it?" Daniel was smiling as his arms tightened around her.

"I'd say the best." He drew quiet, thinking how to explain he had seen Andrew as they both were filling their vehicles at the station and Andrew had learned troubling information from his partner, Pookie.

"You're quiet," she said. Pulling back she knew there was something coming that would cause unrest in their world again and the group was strained these weeks of pulling together and trying to take up slack for one another. "I know we are almost at wit's end but tell me so we can pray about the solution."

"Are the children all right? I don't hear anyone stirring."

"Ruthie took them out to swing, I'd say they will be starving when they come in, but not worn down, yet." She took his hand and led him to the table. "Now, what's on your mind?"

"I ran into Andrew." He saw her expression change to alarm. "No, no, they're fine. Just happy to be home with the children and he did send his love to you." Daniel blew out a breath of air. "Where to begin, I guess first to say, Britany has made Pookie leave. Seems she is on one of those tangents, and whereas they used to be dull and lifeless and noncommitive, now she is going through the screaming and hollering phase," he paused to think and then said, "she lost the baby right at nine months." He sighed, tiredly. "I can't understand how a woman overcomes such heartache and disappointment to carry a baby full term and then lose it." He felt Ellen's questions. "I know, but she turned away from Pookie, told him he needed to leave they were both better off without each other, she didn't need him."

"When she needs him most she makes him leave? That doesn't make sense."

"It didn't make sense that she tried to take Andrew's child, either. She and the second daughter are at odds and she and Mrs. Walden, according to Pookie have no use for each other. So, Britany has pretty much cut herself off from anyone who might care for her, considering circumstances."

"It never ends, does it? I suppose Pookie is concerned for her life." Ellen considered the past when Walden gave Britany drugs and her struggle to overcome the pain of losing her parents threw her into depression. Daniel nodded. "All we can do is pray, isn't it?"

"I wish that were all, but Andrew feels this is a far reaching situation, that she in resentment and rebellion will create turmoil wherever she turns and Pookie loves her but is helpless to do anything constructive. For some strange reason when she turns to such unrest in her soul she finds satisfaction in causing Marigold pain and will stop at nothing to try to destroy Matt in his marriage."

"Their marriage."

"Yes, but you know what I mean, Britany feels she owns Matt and his mother aids and abets her."

"This is troubling. I hoped if Evan come out of this coma, for lack of a better word, that our world would right itself and we could truly see light at the end of the tunnel." Hearing commotion outside the window Ellen glanced across to see Ruthie, little soldier that she was, marching the children in for dinner. "Here they come, our darlings," Ellen quipped. "Want to help sit dinner on the table, daddy of the year?" She rose up to quickly peck a kiss on his lips. "More of that later," she grinned. "That was pretty good."

"Oh, yeah," quickly he took her in his arms and planted a smoldering kiss on her lips. Finished, he said, "You were supposed to faint to the floor, momma of the year."

"Then, who would sit dinner on the table?"

Later, when the children were asleep in their beds and they were turning in, Ellen said, "I can't get Britany off my mind. I know there's a destructive bent to her and I wonder if it's always been there ."

"One thing for sure, Andrew thinks Anne has all she can handle without Britany causing more, but if Britany concentrates on

Marigold and Matt...I don't know...did we sign on for this?" He pulled her close. "I am dog-tired, how about you?"

"I think we should praise the Lord that Evan woke up and ask his guidance in everything else."

* * * * * *

Andrew stepped outside the door knowing Anne was checking on the apartment Jewel and Evan would return to. He heard her footsteps on the path and stepped into the light so he wouldn't scare her. "Can't sleep, Mrs. Graves?"

She gave a slight chuckle, "No, sir, Mr. Graves and you are a fine one to point that out. Why are you up?"

"I knew when you left the bed. Are you worrying over Britany?"

"No. I figure like in the past she will concentrate on Marigold and Matt, but you know what...I think our group must pray more and cast out demons. She is not flying under our heavenly father's flag, now is she? If she has vengeance and unrest in her soul, Britany is behaving other than as someone saved and set aside."

He locked the door behind them. "You sound more like Ellen every day. I give up, what's the plan, evidently you have one. By the way, what were you doing out there?"

"Making the bed with fresh sheets, vacuuming and dusting, that's all and yes, I think we have a plan."

"Woman, it is nearly midnight and I know you are tired. I don't do half the physical work you do and I am." He reached for her hand. "Please, come to bed and tell me what you've decided in the morning."

"Just one more thing, Andrew, I need to put a set of clothes in the washer."

"Anne, please, I don't rest good without you."

She smiled, thinking it wasn't always that way. Instead, she said, "that makes me happy to hear you say it." She turned toward the bedroom. "I did say whither thou goest, I will go, didn't I?"

Andrew groaned. "I loved the young Anne when we were young; I shiver when I admit I mistreated you. Thank God I finally saw my terrible mistake and ask your forgiveness, but now I don't know what to do with the Anne that has grown so strong in the love of the Lord." He sit on the side of the bed, his head in his hands. "Now you make decisions, tell me what's what and I am in such shock…to think you took in Addy and love her as your own." He sighed, swinging his body around onto the mattress. "What's next? I think you should prepare me."

Anne was laughing. "You are a lawyer. For heaven's sakes, we're home. We almost lost everything had it not been for your friend the Judge and we both heard him say, "go home and be thankful I'm still watching out for you." She used the Judge's deep voice. "How did we end up so blessed, Andrew, Harriet and the Judge and our sweet little family. God is good." Now she was coughing for the effort.

"Go to sleep, Anne." Andrew pulled her close, nuzzling the back of her neck. "Honestly, you are killing me and…" his voice was a near whisper, "I love it…I love you..I guess I'll pay for my mistakes the rest of my life…" He was talking but he was asleep. "Maybe someday I'll be as strong in the faith as you…"

* * * * * *

Ruthie awakened from sleep, at least she thought she had been asleep but there was a deep peace surrounding her as she thought on the dream she experienced. Evan was all right for now. There would be complications only time would take care of and Jewel would be by his side. God was granting them the life together they'd hoped for, and then there was Anne and Andrew, Ruthie laughed because in her dream God had shown a side of the two that was funny. Andrew who had always been the domineering one was actually listening to Anne and he seemed happier than Ruthie had ever seen him.

That wasn't all she learned from the dream, if truly God was speaking to her as in times past he spoke to his people, he had included Britany. The last time she dreamed of Britany, God had given her a mission to go to Britany and sit with her, holding her hand while his peace that passes understanding flowed into Britany's heart. Now Britany was sad and there was something she didn't know that perhaps God intended Ruthie to tell her. Obediently, Ruthie accepted the dream as her heart overflowed with joy that he would use her in his kingdom's work. "I'm only seven, heavenly Father," she whispered. I know, he replied in that silent voice only hearts hear, a wonderful age. I have plans for you, Ruthie. It won't always be easy but I'll always be with you. She felt his love as she drifted back to sleep. Tomorrow, she must see Britany. How would God work that out, she wondered, when she was seven and couldn't drive.

*   *   *   *   *   *

"I am alone. Alone. Do you hear me?" Britany stood on the balcony of the old house. She had spent a fortune refurbishing it. The balcony was the next thing to a widow's walk from the old homes built the last century. "Am I to be a widow? Do you want me to throw myself down and make my husband a widower?" She had screamed the day long, driving Pookie away, scaring the hired help so they went home early. "I am sick of myself. Do you hear me up there in your heaven?" She studied the stars, the milky way was showing tonight, like a spider web winding across the sky. "Did you put the stars in the sky to prove you are God?" She ask, her voice beginning to go hoarse. "Why am I so retched I drive people away? He loves me and I've drove him away."

She turned back to enter the room they'd shared. He wasn't a bad husband; it was she who was a bad wife. She lost the baby. It wasn't his but he was willing to claim the baby and be his father. Now there was no baby. Her mind was in torment, her body in agony and if she had a heart it must be black as stone. Was she demon possessed? Was it the drugs Clayton fed to her to keep her in obedience to him? Before she shut the door, she stared up into the sky. "If you are real, if you are the God of our Father's, the one who created the world and all that is in it, I will acknowledge you if you will send someone to me. I need someone. Do you understand? Send me flesh and blood with a caring heart. Tomorrow."

Drained of all energy she fell across the bed and slept while the night slipped into day and the farm came alive as though nothing of significance happened the day before, except the man who usually walked with the dog and fed the horses was not there. There was no stirring on the balcony where the woman screamed and hollered the day before and the hired help wondered if all was well.

Pookie had been summoned by Daniel. Stiff with anticipation, he feared Daniel would tell him Britany finally committed the act she had threatened the last months since losing the baby. Andrew called him to ask would he go by the Gates house, Daniel would be waiting and Ruthie. Why Ruthie?

He pulled into the drive, noticing next door the three older women were out in the yard. They kept to themselves, according to Andrew, though the grapevine spread word they were wealthy beyond means, a bit eccentric but friendly. What a description, he thought, considering they'd been there nearly a year. They waved to him and he waved back.

Formalities of greeting and small talk preceded his being ask to take a seat. "Is everything all right?" He finally blurted out.

"Yes, it is," Daniel replied. "But Ruthie had an unusual dream last night in which she felt compelled to see Britany. We were wondering, would you be so kind as to accompany her to see your wife?"

"I'm sure you've heard Britany is on a rampage and yet you would entrust me to take your daughter to see her?"

Daniel smiled. "You might say the Lord has governed this. Has Britany told you about when she and Ruthie met? If not, trust me, it was good and this meeting will be also."

"If you say so." Pookie rose up from sitting. "I'll be happy to drive Ruthie. Britany is most unhappy."

It was the strangest request Pookie had experienced in life. He knew a little about Ruthie. There was a rumor she was gifted, by that it was explained God had given her a gift of bringing peace where there was turmoil and he could use that himself. "I understand your friend who lost everything in the flood has regained consciousness," he said, deciding small talk might be necessary.

"You mean Evan," she replied. "Would you like to hear Evan's story? It might help you understand how God works in mysterious ways and will again, I believe today, or he would not have told me to visit Britany." Pookie nodded. "I will begin with sitting in church and God showed me a picture in my mind of Evan," she began. "I don't know why I'm used this way, maybe it is His way of bringing people into our lives. My momma has this gift and she says we must always listen and do only what God tells us."

By the time Ruthie finished her story and they arrived at the farm, there was hope in Pookie's heart.

"The missus has not awakened," the housekeeper informed him.

"Allow this young lady to go up to her room," he said. "Things will be better." The woman looked doubtful.

Ruthie found Britany sleeping soundly. "She looks pale," she said to the housekeeper.

"She should," the woman replied, "all that hollerin' and screamin' she did yesterday."

"You may leave me alone with her, we are friends." Shaking her head the woman went away.

Ruthie crawled upon the bed beside Britany and took her hand into her own. "Do you know how many times I've ridden with someone to see a person because that's what I have to do when our heavenly Father tells me to?" Ruthie continued talking. "Do you remember when you fell on the street and Marigold and Matt rescued you? it was the day we were doing praise in the park where Pastor Levi and Leah live. I held your hand and you told me later you felt rest that you hadn't had for weeks. I think you are tired, again. But I have something wonderful to tell you. Have your forgotten God loves you? The lady said you've been busy hollering and screaming. I think you have felt pain, maybe because you lost your momma and daddy. Or maybe you are sad losing your little baby. God knows all about your pain and what you have lost. Did you forget? I feel sad now that you have been so miserable. I would have sit with you and listened to anything you wanted to tell me. I'm just a kid but I listen really good. Now, I'm going to put my arm around you and just love you the way Jesus wants us to love each other. I'm just seven years old but He puts such joy in my heart. I don't understand a lot of things but I do know the difference between being happy or sad and having peace and joy in my heart. I pray now, Britany, as I lay beside you that God visits you in your dreams and tells you the exciting news he has for you. I really feel he will because all our friends at home are praying for you while I'm here with you, too."

* * * * * *

CHAPTER 16

"God does work in mysterious ways, his wonders to perform," Ellen whispered into Daniel's ear as they sit in Christ Church the next Sunday. "Evidently, all Britany needs to get her started on the right track back to being healthy is a friend and Ruthie is willing to be her friend but I'm thinking Ruthie's work is over. It seems Jewel has been drawn to befriend Britany. It seems both Evan and Jewel have experienced life in a different way than the rest of us and understand the awkwardness of Britany and Pookie's nature."

"Do I understand Britany is willing to go for counseling and Pookie also if their marriage needs it?"

"That's what we've heard through Jewel and Evan. If Evan's home is considered unlivable according to the county rules, there's a house on Britany's property that she has offered for them to live in." Ellen sighed, contently. "I don't know if you heard us talking but Evan said for the first time he feels contentment in his life, not just through Jewel though she's the largest contributor but he felt the first time he saw little Addy that God had included him as part of a plan to protect that child. He didn't understand in the beginning but now he does and it made him happy to help someone else."

"I remember Evan saying some live for a moment of fame but he feels there are many like himself that are born for a moment in time and his time was when he was able to bring Addy home to Andrew and Anne." He turned to face Ellen, "What was the news Ruthie had for Britany? I forgot to ask."

Ellen beamed. "Britany is expecting another baby and this one belongs to her husband. That made her realize she had to be healthy in mind, body and spirit. Do you see them sitting three rows from the front?" Daniel glanced to where she mentioned. "Isn't God good," Ellen said, "to all of us?"

"I'm looking forward to a worship service that is peaceful and serene. We have way too much drama."

"Oh, daddy of the year, that's how it is when you love the Lord, he keeps things moving."

Ellen scanned the rows in front of them; the group were all present. "Yes, God is good, very good," she whispered. Daniel leaned over to kiss the top of her head.

The END